ALSO BY JAN SURASKY

Rage Against the Dying Light

Back to Jerusalem

The Lilac Bush Is Blooming

THE SOUND

OF

UNHEARD MELODIES

THE SOUND

OF

UNHEARD MELODIES

A NOVEL

JAN SURASKY

Published by Sandalwood Press
Victor, New York

Cover and Interior Design by Susan Surasky
Larkspur Design

Library of Congress Cataloging-in-Publication Card Number:
TXu2-149-570

*To those who have shared their kindnesses
with the world*

Special Dedication

This page is dedicated to Mike, a Native American who was sent from the Tonawanda reservation in Buffalo, New York to our high school in Rochester. The Tonawanda reservation was mired in poverty and its education facilities substandard.

Mike was handsome, shy, kind and generous of spirit. He was my friend and a friend to all our classmates. As summer vacation approached, Mike confided to me one day he was not looking forward to returning to the reservation for the summer break because the reservation was hot, depressing, run down, with no amenities and especially, I suppose, no hope for the future.

But, a conflict raged within him. He so very much was looking forward to seeing his mother who lived on the reservation and who, he confided, he loved so very much.

In our junior year Mike who, it was obvious, could never resolve that conflict took his own life.

We lost a friend but his tormented soul lives on in all of us.

Heard melodies are sweet, but those unheard
are sweeter...

-John Keats

"...THE LILIES OF THE FIELD WHOSE BLOOM IS
BRIEF—WE ARE AS THEY..."

-Christina Rossetti

"A LILY NEVER PRETENDS...ITS BEAUTY IS THAT IT
IS WHAT IT IS."

-Jiddu Krishnamurti

Acknowledgments

My thanks to all who have shared their knowledge of the history and culture and customs of the Cherokee people, from museums and libraries to individuals who have cared enough to document the customs, the beliefs, the rites that have been carried down through the centuries, and demonstrations of the wonderful cooking of their ancestors.

My thanks also to the museums and libraries that have provided material on the Victorian era, the history of Boston and Oklahoma.

Appreciation to the Romani people for sharing their history and the beautiful and colorful music traditions of a people once commonly known as gypsies.

Also, for the many stray articles on the internet that lovingly told the story of Oklahoma from the advent of the railroads to the experience of traversing the ancient forest floor of the amazing and unique Cross Timbers.

A special thanks to those who critiqued this manuscript and provided encouragement and support and were there when I needed them most my deepest gratitude.

THE SOUND

OF

UNHEARD MELODIES

Chapter One

H er name was Lily. She was named that because as a child her mother had often sought comfort in the woodlands near her home among the beautiful, wild lilies-of-the-valley, a flower that blooms only in May and gives off a most delicious scent.

For her mother, whose name was Elena, it was a welcome escape from the hardscrabble life her family was forced to live. Her mother was of Spanish heritage and her ancestors, though welcome in their adopted country of America, the country they chose to flee to at a time of oppression in their native Spain, never quite fit in. They had never been gentry in their homeland, and they didn't quite know how to grab onto the dream their new land claimed to offer.

Nevertheless, although they had jobs that seemed never to work out, and scratching from the land seemed always to be futile, they managed to feed the many mouths that came along. They were not cultured like the many European immigrants that populated their new land, but they managed to survive and even have fun after the long hard days.

Unlike those who also staked a claim in many of the new territories going west, they were loud and boisterous, they liked to dance the Flamenco to the homemade guitars they often fashioned after long days in the fields, and the elders always found a way to make moonshine after dark.

Although Elena loved her many brothers and sisters and loved helping her Mama sew clothes from the flour sacks they saved and dyed with the beautiful flowers of the woodland she was determined to do better. She would marry a rich man and save her whole family from the poverty they had endured for centuries.

Elena was beautiful but she was also smart. When she was allowed to take the one old horse the family had possessed for years to pull the plow and a small wagon to purchase the few items they were able to get in town by bargaining she managed to wheedle a length of ribbon or a small hand-carved soldier for one of her brothers from Hiram Aston who owned the only general store in town by entertaining him with stories she made up by the hour.

She also found her way to the old schoolhouse behind the church where the families who were better off sent their children since they didn't need them to plow fields or dip candles or pump water or help with the many chores it took to keep a small log cabin as spruced up as it could be or walk behind an old simple plow when seeding time came or chop wood like her brothers did.

At the schoolhouse she hung back until the children had all left for the day or were out of doors for recess. It was then that she would sneak in to talk to the schoolmaster. He was a young man and could easily see Elena's plight and eventually took pity on her when he could see she had a big thirst for knowledge and nowhere to slake it. He taught her to read and began slipping her some old tattered books he had acquired and taught her her sums when she was ready. And so through the years Elena became as educated as the other children who arrived at the schoolhouse in pretty dresses and handsome britches.

When Elena was eighteen true to her word she attracted the attention of a middle-aged bachelor who had never married and spent his life up until then accumulating wealth and having nowhere to spend it or the inclination to do so.

He was smitten with her and dazzled by her

intelligence and her beauty. They were married immediately and he built her a very large house in the mountains far from town with all the trimmings. There were very large shutters in the Spanish style her ancestors had handed down memories of, and gilt-framed mirrors all over for Elena to admire herself in.

Elena was not vain, but she did like to primp. And, she liked to dance the Flamenco in the evening hours after the day's work was done. Not that she worked that hard, but she did have to see to it that the floors were scrubbed and the linens ironed and put away.

Her husband, whose name was Alfred R. Paxton, liked to watch her dance, so he brought in a Victrola from a very large city many miles away so she could have her Flamenco music. He also brought in some servants so she wouldn't have to work so hard because he liked her soft hands and her delicate countenance so she worked very hard to please him and used all manner of creams to soften her beautiful olive skin so reminiscent of her Spanish gypsy ancestors.

From the day of their marriage her family never had to scratch food from the land again but were bought new plows and two oxen to pull them and a cow to give milk and a hen to lay eggs and a new churn to turn the cream into butter. Her brothers and sisters wore store bought clothes and her Mama had a pretty dress and new bonnet for Sunday church.

And into all this Lily was born.

Lily was a beautiful baby with delicate milky white skin and a tuft of brownish hair that seemed to defy description and blend in with the earth itself. She was as delicate as the lovely white bells of her namesake that fluttered gently in the May spring breezes.

Elena thought her beautiful the minute she arrived in the world and gave her everything a baby could want. She had a cradle imported from France along with the most intricate baby blankets and hand-made caps and lace dresses. She would rock her and sing her to sleep with lullabies she had heard and dance the Flamenco with her in her arms when she wakened.

Alfred was more distant and left all her care to Elena. He was frightened of newborns and most of all had no interest. But, when she was five or six they became inseparable, overseeing his mines in the mountains together and checking on his other business interests which were many.

He would whisk her out of bed in the morning and

get her dressed in her finest. "You must look like we're successful, child. The miners must know who's boss."

And, after a hearty breakfast prepared by a servant but carefully overseen by Elena they would head for the mountains and Alfred's holdings.

Alfred had been lucky in finding wealth under the ground. But, that is not to say he didn't search in the proper manner. He had a knack for sniffing out wealth and as one of the early miners in Oklahoma he had struck it rich. He had found rubies, a rare gem he shipped east to be made into all manner of beautiful jewelry for the wealthy. He had also found coal, a perfect find because it fed the steam engines that were crossing the land on tracks that had yet to be laid to reach the Pacific Ocean.

So Alfred bought a fairly sizable interest in the railroad pushing west. He was rewarded with a sizable profit because the railroad was the hope for this new country's industrial future.

Their buggy pushed along at a rapid pace drawn by two of the liveliest red roans in the territory. Down they went toward the prairie grasses and up the foothills of the nearby mountain that was a treasure trove of gems and coal and all manner of riches to be pulled from the earth and shipped back east to buy silks and satins and ribbons and bows and all manner of beautiful cherry wood furniture for Elena to fill the house with.

"Papa, may I get out and pick a bouquet?"

The pale of the wildflowers with the rays of the sunlight dancing among them still wet with dew never ceased to fascinate Lily and she longed to run through the early morning prairie grasses, their untamed greens and golds still rustling in the soft breezes that seemed always to accompany the vivid pinks, the scarlets, and the long brilliant swatches of orange of an Oklahoma sky at daybreak.

"We have to get on so we can get to the mines before the men. Although we're lucky to have the miners we have, they're a dedicated lot, and they've been loyal through the years, they need direction and they value it. We need to pull what we can before the claim jumpers start arriving to put us out of business or Oklahoma is opened to settlers from the east.

"Right now, the Indians leave us alone. They're not interested in mining. They're buffalo hunters and they like the freedom of the prairies."

Lily never understood what Alfred was trying to

tell her about business but she always listened politely because she didn't want to hurt his feelings. And, she knew he was a man of great pride. She watched Mama listen intently to his stories of the mines and the railroads and how they would get rich and Mama could have anything she wanted.

Mama would sit at his feet at night and glance up at him with the greatest of admiration. Lily would play quietly with her dolls as they talked. She would dress them up in their finery and take them to great balls or to call on the most important people in Washington or even the kings and queens of Europe where she would surely travel someday and which she had seen in a photograph book cherished by her latest governess Mama had hired to educate Lily and turn her into the fine lady Elena had always yearned to be.

The sun broke through as the sunrise receded into the blue of the sky. As they broke through the dense forest filled with short, stubby post oak, tall, majestic pines, redcedar and flowering dogwood, and as they climbed the mountain, Lily could hear the robins chattering about as they chased their morning meal.

"Here we are," announced Alfred, as he pulled the horses to a stop and got out to hitch them to the post where his tobacco-chewing assistant Hector would care for them during the day, making sure they had enough feed and water, and an occasional rare carrot or lump of sugar which he always gave to Lily whenever she was about.

"Mornin', Lily."

"Good morning, Mr. Hector. Can I feed the horses today?"

"Of course. I wouldn't have it any other way. And, if you look in the station on the desk, there's a wooden ball my Jamie carved for you. Now mind you don't go losin' it down those hills."

"I won't Mr. Hector. Can I see it now?"

"Of course. But mind you keep checking the sky. It's starting to look like a storm and you need to take cover in the station. You never know whether a tornado might be kicking up."

As Hector helped her out of the buggy she patted the horses, making sure to call them by the secret names she had given them. Although Alfred never named his horses, Lily was certain they would never get to heaven without a name.

As Lily's feet touched the ground she ran for the station, anxious to see the ball Jamie had carved especially for her.

Jamie was her friend even though she had seen him only once. He had arrived with Hector at the mine at a time when the mine was especially lush, its veins giving up plentiful ore and the miners beside themselves with glee. Alfred always shared the wealth and it meant a big bonus.

"Who are you?" he had asked, as Lily stared up at the tall, handsome lad, stunned at his good looks, but overwhelmed at his outfit, since he was as fastidious as Hector was not.

"I'm Jamie. Who are you?"

"I'm Lily."

"Oh, you're Mr. Paxton's girl. I better watch out how I treat you. I'll get in a pack of trouble with my Pa if I don't let you win at rollin' the wagon wheel or let you catch me at tag or hide and seek. Or let you win at a game of marbles."

"You don't have to let me win. I can beat you. I know I can. I play lots of games with my dolls and I always win."

"Oh, yeah? Girls can't play marbles. My sisters sniffle if I beat them. But, I beat them every time."

Jamie pulled some marbles from the brown woolen

britches he wore tucked into the leather boots he had fashioned himself. He threw them on the floor. There two larger marbles stood out from the rest of the pack.

"Those two big ones are the shooters. You can choose. What color do you want?"

Lily took a long time to look over the crop of beautifully polished marbles. "I'll take the green one. It's the color of the prairie grasses."

"Okay. My red will beat your green every time."

"No, it won't. You'll see."

Lily wasn't certain whether Jamie ended up letting her win or whether she won because of the skill she had found when Alfred got her toys meant for boys. He insisted on teaching her boys' games against the wishes of Elena who wanted to make a fine lady out of her when what he wanted was for her to take over his businesses when she became of age.

She only knew she was struck by his good looks and that he was so much older than she was but he still took the time to take her seriously.

Jamie was surrounded by sisters and they teased him mercilessly. They also spoiled him when circumstances and the work on their very small farm allowed.

They would bake his favorite cornbread or cherry pie. They would find tidbits of extra succulent roasted rabbit that he had brought down in the endless quest for small game to fill their table to tempt him with.

Lily did neither. She considered everyone who crossed her path an equal because as an only child her companions were adults and they treated her like an equal because they had no idea how else to treat her.

In the afternoon, Jamie and Lily wandered the dense forests that surrounded the mine. Jamie was intent upon showing Lily how to make a bow and arrow from a sapling tree and how to chase a rabbit into his hole as he skittered back and forth to fool an enemy.

Jamie was anxious to show Lily his knowledge of forest trees. He knew the oaks and the sycamores and the pines and the redcedars. He knew what would make a sturdy chair or a big table to eat upon or a chest of drawers to hold the beautiful dresses and britches his Ma sewed even by candlelight when the day's chores were done.

Lily looked up to the sky but saw none. "Where did the sky go?"

Jamie laughed. "The tall pines and the elm trees and

the sycamores grow so close they block the light. But, the sky will never go away. It's there forever."

Lily wasn't certain of the concept of forever. But, she wanted to please Jamie so she listened intently to everything he said.

She looked down at the forest floor. "Where are the flowers? The prairie grasses are full of beautiful daisies all white and yellow. And flowers I can pick to make a bouquet out of to take back to Mama with colors the same as my favorite paints that Mama sends for."

"Flowers need sunshine to bloom like people do. The trees of our forests are so close together they practically hug. But, they keep out the sunshine so no flowers throw down their seed 'cause they won't bloom."

Lily began to think that Jamie was the only person she knew who knew everything. And, he treated her more gently than anyone she ever knew.

"Now, let's go see if the robins and chickadees have laid their eggs."

They searched until they found a chickadee nest in a hole in an elm tree, its base the moss of the forest floor, then bits of bark and rabbit fur nestling the newly laid eggs, their dull white covered by reddish brown speckles. "The babies will be born soon," said Jamie. "They'll be fed and cared for until they're ready to fly. But, then they'll be on their own and we'll have more chickadees to fill the forest with song."

The robin's eggs had been laid as well, their soft blue a beautiful contrast to the twigs of the carefully woven nest.

"We'd better get back. Pa will wonder if we've gone off to another territory."

As Lily's thoughts returned to the present, she went into the station to see what Jamie had made especially for her. It was a ball carved from the wood of the majestic pines of the forest polished to a gloss with the fine powder of the weathered Oklahoma limestone. Her name was painted in large, bold letters across the middle.

The miners began to straggle in, some of them walking miles from Indian territory or some from very small cabins where they kept a stock of goods sent for from France or Spain for the lucrative Indian trade.

Lily kept to herself out of the way of the miners as Alfred gave them the day's instructions. Hector checked all of the safety gear and pulled the levers that sent them down to darkness and another day of hope that maybe they'd finally strike a mother lode that would send them all into an easier life for themselves and for their families.

Lily checked the darkening sky through the large, station windows for clouds resembling angels or men on horseback or queens with long flowing robes she had only imagined from the many stories Mama had read or told her. She was certain she would someday meet them all.

Chapter Two

T he Oklahoma skies were threatening rain when Lily edged her way down the mountain top but Lily paid no mind. Oklahoma weather was as unpredictable as Mama when she dropped everything to sing and dance her wild gypsy melodies and begged Lily to join in.

She was one with the pony she was presently astride and threats of rain could not dissuade her from heading for the woods thick with oak and the prairies lush with multi-colored grasses grown tall toward the sun sharing space with the most beautiful and varied wildflowers of the season.

It was here she could run free. She had begged for a pony for her tenth birthday and Papa had granted her wish with a beautiful dapple-gray that stood just ten hands high. But, what he lacked in size he made up in spirit.

She had named him Paco after one of the handymen she had taken a shine to who had come round to fix the loose rafters that Alfred had no time for and to build shelves of absolute elegance for the many dishes and platters Elena was collecting along with the many recipes she found in the ladies' magazines she sent for. Lily and Alfred were often pressed into service tasting new dishes she insisted Cook try on the new cast iron coal stove that she was certain graced the tables of the wealthiest and most fashionable eastern manors.

Lily rode through the prairie grasses bathed in the sun that had suddenly replaced the dark threatening sky. The gold and greens of the grasses were nearly as high as Paco and the beautiful purple of the violet, the pale lavender of the iris, and the purity of the white trout lily all vied for the rays of the sun.

She reached the woods by mid-morning, ready to settle in among the short, gnarly post and blackjack oaks. They were her companions, these trees that stood hundreds of years of drought and deprivation, their prickly bark daunting to all who dared to cross through them.

As she hitched Paco to a tree facing the prairie so he could explore at his leisure, she heard a rustle not far but paid it no mind. Probably a squirrel scampering to find a buried acorn or a red bird hopping from tree to tree to find just the right twig to complete a softly feathered nest.

She spread her blanket beneath a post oak and settled her dolls and a midday meal Cook had packed with tiny little tea sandwiches, strawberry jam and cornbread, and a healthy portion of last night's pot roast which she knew Lily favored.

Lily would have tea with her dolls, tell them stories until meal time, and then head back before supper with bouquets of daisies and primroses for Mama and Cook.

As she sat, not far from a post oak, its gnarly branches looking for all she could see like the arm of the wicked witch in a fable Mama saved to tell without fail around every Halloween campfire, a beautiful Palomino appeared, its white mane and tail, its golden coat brushed to a shine, a boy of about her own age, his long, straight thick hair as dark as the night sky without a star in it, sitting tall and bareback upon it.

"Who are you?"

"I'm Lily. Who are you?"

"I am Wohali."

"But, you are Indian. You must be far from home. Papa says the Indians live far."

"I am not far from home. I do not live with my tribe."

18

"Why do you have no saddle?"

"I do not ride with a saddle. My father taught me to ride on the bare back of a horse when I was very young. 'Without a saddle,' he said, 'you and your horse will be one. He will take you many places and teach you many things. But, he will feel free not like the horse of the white man for he will be as the horses of his own wild herd.'"

Lily looked long at Wohali. He was a strange one, this boy so intense and yet so curious. Not like her many cousins who arrived for Thanksgiving or Christmas. Or whose home, though sparse, was filled with laughter and song. They were always ready to play and include Lily in their silly games and let her help with the chores of which there were many even though she did none at home.

"Would you like to eat a meal with me and my dolls?"

Wohali stared at Lily. "No one has ever asked to share their midday meal with me. Not even William."

"Who is William?"

"William looks after my mother and me when he is around. He traps raccoons and beavers and squirrels and trades with the Choctaws and the Creeks. He lives in a cabin not far from here. My father was gored by a buffalo so I must provide food. I am a good hunter and we grow many vegetables."

Lily stared at Wohali again. She had never known anyone so brave and strong and so old for his years. She was careful to say only what she thought would keep him there for he seemed ready to bolt at the slightest sign of a crackling twig underfoot of a scampering squirrel or the birds chirping too loudly as a sign of trouble.

She pulled two small dishes from her scrolled leather pack and laid them out on her blanket. As she laid the pot roast on one of them and the tea sandwiches on the other, Wohali stared at the small china plates painted with beautiful roses and filled with such goodies. "I shall add some buffalo jerky to your midday meal for it is all I have. But, it will give you energy to ride long on the prairies and through the rough woods and you will not be frightened of the bark of the post or the blackjack oak for the meat and the fat of the buffalo will give you courage."

He dismounted and led his Palomino to a nearby tree. "I must tie Gola to the trunk of a sturdy oak so he does not wander. He is very strong. He will drink the water I have brought him from the stream that runs alongside these woods and perhaps he will sleep. He works hard to carry me to the hunt of squirrels and rabbits and he pulls the small plow I have fashioned to spread the seed of our small field.

"I must care well for Gola. Before we had a horse my father and his fathers hunt buffalo on foot. Buffalo are fast and many people starve."

Wohali settled himself on the blanket and began to pull pieces of the leftover pot roast that Lily pushed toward him. Sensing his enjoyment Lily took the tea sandwiches for herself and shared the cornbread and strawberry jam.

Wohali pulled buffalo jerky from his small pack. "You must eat these. They give you energy for all your journeys."

Lily looked at the strips of salted meat, dried as the ancients to keep the hard-won meat of the hunt and so unlike the refined dishes Mama placed at table. As each strip crackled and crunched beneath her teeth, she was certain she could taste upon her tongue the earth, the stars, the whole of the universe.

As suddenly as he had appeared, Wohali jumped up. "I must go. I must fell the game and gather the firewood before sundown."

"But, will I see you again?"

"I am here often. I will look for you."

As Wohali rode off, as quietly as he had come, the earthen floor of the forest, with the exception of a few crackling twigs, seemed almost silent, the woods suddenly empty despite the chase of the squirrels and the rabbits, and the song of the birds nattering about in their confusion of a late afternoon.

Lily picked up her blanket and placed her dolls in their carrying case. She packed up her leather pouch and untied Paco. They must hurry for the skies were darkening.

As they crossed the prairies, the wildflowers thirsting for rain, Lily's thoughts were filled only with Wohali. But, she urged Paco to go faster. They mustn't be late for supper.

Chapter Three

L ily was wishing the horses could go faster as she and Mama and Papa and Enrico the hired man headed in their finest oaken and pinewood sleigh across the plains and through the rough timbered forests to Grandmama Manuela's house. Enrico had come along to help drive the sleigh while Lily and Elena sat in the back to mind the many gifts Elena always insisted on lavishing on Grandmama and her many nieces and nephews but he was always glad to be asked since he had no kin west of the Carolinas and looked forward to Grandmama's home cooking and her way with a turkey.

Grandmama Manuela was not like the doting grandmothers in the picture books that Mama had sent for to educate Lily in the finer things in life. She was very slender and loved to dance as Elena did. She let her hair fly about her as she danced and the clashes of the many bangles she wore on her wrists helped keep time to the music just as well as the timpani player of a very large formal orchestra.

Grandmama Manuela loved to pose riddles to Lily

and to fill the hours they were together with tales of her gypsy ancestors she had only heard about. Lily listened patiently as she imagined a country so different from the rough terrain of Oklahoma, gypsy fiddles and campfires, and spirited horses.

Today was Thanksgiving and all Mama's relatives would fill the small cabin around a large, oak table that was a gift from Mama when she married Papa. Grandmama had a beautiful, large oven to roast the turkey in and Lily knew the table would be filled with the bounty of the field, the corn and beans, the turnips, the parsnips and the pumpkins her cousins worked so hard to sow, thin the seedlings, plow and hoe, and finally pull from a sometimes unforgiving earth.

Thanksgiving was special at Grandmama's house. Mama was bringing two pies and a sweet potato casserole that she had Cook make from a recipe that she was certain was part of the very first Thanksgiving celebration at Plymouth. Mama liked history because it showed off her learning and she felt it her duty to share what she knew with her brothers and sisters who had little book learning. But, although they listened politely they were happiest in the fields turning the soil, walking behind the plow to make neat, even furrows in land they had found near Grandmama's, and praying silently for the sun and the rain to come in equal measure to nurture the golden wheat, the hay and the feed corn and the peanuts and cotton that often fed and clothed the nearby townsfolk.

The rough, mineral-rich Oklahoma territory was plagued by growing pains. Civil War veterans, both of the north and the south, Indians and white settlers alike, had not healed their pain. The greed of the railroads threatened the Indian land grants and forced the tribes to turn on each other. And, with all this, Elena's brothers were certain that what they saw as a bright future if they worked hard in the fields would finally break the cycle of ancestral poverty that had plagued their family for generations.

Lily looked about the sleigh as they rode. The prairies were covered with a blanket of snow and the wildflowers nowhere to be seen. Lily was certain they were asleep and dreaming of what beautiful colors they would become when the birds arrived to fill the air with song and the soft spring breezes and gentle rains, along with the warmth of the sun, would nurture their buds.

"Mama, will cousin Lita be there?"

"Of course, Lily. She will be there with Uncle Luis and Aunt Maria and her little brothers and sisters and their new baby Daniel. Perhaps you and Lita can bundle him up and take him for a sleigh ride in the sleigh we are bringing for him as a christening gift."

"Can we go to the hills, Mama?"

"Of course, but mind you get him back so he can suckle. He will be hungry you know."

"We will, Mama."

Lily's cousin Carmelita, known as Lita from birth for her flashing dark eyes that lit up when she laughed as she often did, was her favorite. As gay and full of laughter as Lily was reserved and somber, Lita brought joy to Lily's otherwise rather drab existence. They often went off together with Lily's dolls to giggle over trivial things as girls their age did or share their secrets and dreams for the future.

"We're here," shouted father, as Enrico urged the horses on the last lap that brought them over the hill to Grandmama's small cabin. Grandpapa, who Lily had never known, had been lost to an Oklahoma twister but Grandmama spoke endlessly of him, how strong he was and how they had loved each other since childhood, as tears fell from her wide brown eyes that stood out beneath the glitter of a length of silver hair that always managed to escape from the many shell combs she placed in it, and over her olive, high-boned cheeks weathered from years of struggle behind a primitive plow that gave hope every spring of a bountiful table.

As the horses slowed Uncle Mario ran from the cabin, a big grin on his face and a hug for Elena and a big bear hug for Lily that nearly crushed her along with a more serious handshake for Papa and a pat on the back for Enrico as he took the reins to lead the horses to the big, wooden barn for a bag of feed and a rest. Uncle Mario was big and mustachioed with muscles that bulged from his arms but he was the gentlest of the uncles and always found a way to smuggle some extra sweets for Lily when no one was looking or find an extra hug for Elena who as the youngest of her brothers still looked up to her as his big sister.

As Lily waited patiently for Mama to gather up the gifts and for Enrico to lift her down the door of the cabin burst open and Lita, nearly a foot taller than when Lily saw her last, or so it seemed, came running at a speed that would test the swiftest coyote.

"Cousin, cousin," she shouted, as she ran for the sleigh, her thick dark hair flying in the wind, her slender body, almost a copy of Grandmama's, borne on feet that seemed suddenly to have sprouted wings. "I couldn't wait 'til you got here. We have so much to talk about. I made so many things for you."

Lily's heart warmed as she heard Lita's voice. Lita was her cousin but she was also her best friend. As Enrico helped her down she had her arms out for an embrace but Lita was already at her side. "I have so much to tell you too, Lita. I have made a wonderful friend I met in the woods. He is so different but I know you would like him too."

"I wanted to be the first to show you our new baby brother Daniel but Mama says I must wait 'til he wakes from his nap. He smiles and gurgles all day and doesn't mind when we play hide and seek with him but he gives away our hiding places and he's no good at tag because he can't run yet. But, he doesn't mind coming along when we play hoops and we carry him along in his wagon. Mama says when he gets to be three he'll probably outrun us all he's so strong already."

Lita paused, out of breath. "I can't wait to show you my new doll Papa made for me. I named her Lily."

Lily walked toward the cabin, Lita alongside. As she burst through the pine door, its knob fashioned from more sturdy oak, Grandmama stood waiting to throw her arms around her and squeeze her until she nearly burst. "Lily, you have grown so tall. You are nearly a young lady now. Your mama has done a fine job with all that fancy schooling. I'm sure I have no riddles left that you won't be able to find an answer to."

Lily looked at Grandmama, her hair frazzled, beads of perspiration forming across her brow, but to Lily she was the most beautiful woman she had ever seen. Lily could only see her dancing with her bangles jangling, her tambourine keeping time to the music she loved. "Grandmama, when will Daniel be up?"

"I think I hear him now, Lily. I'm sure he is waiting to go with you and Carmelita to the hills."

Then, Grandmama left the stove to turn her attention to Mama, throwing her arms around her with kisses and hugs, obvious in her pride toward her eldest. "Elena, you look beautiful. Caring for Alfred and Lily must agree with you."

"Alfred is bringing in the pies, Mama. Enrico can help Luis and Mario chop the wood for the fire. Maria and I can warm the sweet potato casserole."

Grandmama beamed as she looked upon Elena. She had never lost her pleasure in watching her eldest be a wife to a man who was in her eyes such a success and raise so carefully a daughter to fit into the circles of the finest drawing rooms in the east. She was certain Lily would achieve what had slipped through the grasp of her many ancestors before her, despite their good intentions.

As Lily and Lita pulled Daniel in his new sleigh toward the hills, Lita was agog with excitement. "We had a good harvest this year, Lily. The first one we've really ever had. Mama said there's enough money to buy me some yards of blue silk. I already picked it out at the general store in town when we went in to sell our cotton to the ladies who buy from us for their spinning wheels and turn the threads into lengths of fabrics to send east where they're turned into the most beautiful garments. I've seen pictures in catalogs at the general store. Mr. Peterson says the fabric's mine even if he has to wait for the money."

"What fashion will your blue silk dress be?"

"I haven't decided yet. Mr. Peterson says the latest catalogs will be coming in soon and he will save them for me. I think I'll wait till then so I can have the latest fashion. I can't wait till I can wear it to church. I know everyone in the schoolhouse will be envious."

"Mama has the latest fashion magazines from Europe. I can save them for you so when we have our big Christmas dinner and everyone is there we can sneak off and you can pick."

"Oh, would you, Lily? Then I can have a dress that no one else will have, not even that rich girl in town who always has the latest fashions from back east. Maybe then she won't have all the boys around her like she does now."

"Pay her no mind, Lita. You are the most beautiful girl I know. Those boys should discover that soon."

Lita threw her arms around Lily. "Oh, Lily, you always know what to say."

Lita paused, then spoke. "When I grow up I want to marry a rich man like your Mama. Then maybe I can have a house like yours and a beautiful new sleigh and stables and clothes from Europe.

"What do you want to be, Lily?"

"I never paid it any mind. Papa wants me to take over the mines and Mama wants me to be a fine lady and go back east to the drawing rooms and find a man who wants to be president or maybe sail to Europe to find a nobleman. But, I'm not sure what I want.

"When I grow up I want to change the world. I want to put lots of buffalo in the world so the Indians don't starve and I want to make crops grow big and tall. Jamie says they barely made their harvest last year and I hardly get to see him because he is so busy hoeing and keeping the pests away."

"I know you'll do it, Lily. You have so much book learning.

"I'll race you back to the cabin and I'll even pull Daniel at the same time."

Lily giggled at Lita's determination but she decided to save her own news for another time. Lita had a harder life than she did, working the fields, caring for the little ones, and so little time for her studies. Lily always wanted to make their time together special.

The day went more quickly than Lily could have imagined. The table was bursting with the bountiful harvest of the fall and the little ones fell promptly asleep after the feast in front of the fire which was now a fierce blaze thanks to the pinewood Enrico had split which looked like it would last Grandmama till Christmas. The women washed and wiped Grandmama's good dishes which Grandpapa had travelled many miles to the nearest town to purchase as a special surprise to celebrate their tenth harvest together while the men fell asleep in the sparse collection of chairs after a good smoke.

Lily was quiet on the way home, the night sky clear, the stars twinkling around a full moon. A heavy blanket kept the chill of the night air from Lily while she counted the stars they left behind. Every star reminded her of Wohali and she was certain he was looking down upon her. He had left for the buffalo hunt with William and would not be back for a fortnight. Nevertheless, she was planning their next adventures together and keeping in her head all the stories she was so anxious to share. As drowsiness won over her determination to stay awake for the rest of the journey she prayed only that he be safe.

Chapter Four

P aco trotted across the prairie grasses grown high with the gentle spring rains, muzzle bobbing, his mane flying in the occasional gusts of brisk winds that swept across the Oklahoma plains as he carried Lily to the Cross Timber woods she favored. The big drifts of winter had kept him in as a stable horse and he was glad to be released into the bursts of sunlight upon his back and pretend to nip at the rabbits and squirrels as they passed.

Spring had brought the beauty of the wildflower blossoms to the prairies once again. The soft yellow of the wood sorrel, the deep golden yellow of the black-eyed Susan, and the pale lavender of the purple iris.

Lily was anxious to see if Wohali had returned from the buffalo hunt and if he would be in the woods chasing the small game that kept his mother and himself from hunger while she labored behind the plow hewn from the rough-barked post oak his father had built to loosen the soil and plant the seed that they both hoped would bring them a bountiful harvest and much corn for his mother to pound into meal for bread that would keep them through the winter.

As they reached the forest, Lily dismounted to tie Paco to one of the blackjack oaks that edged the dark woods, its ancient, gnarly trunk standing sturdy despite years of drought and the unrelenting forces of a wind-whipping tornado. She tied on a bag of feed and assured him she would not forget the cool, clear water of the stream that edged the nearby thicket.

She pulled from her pack a thick wool blanket, the jams and scones Cook had baked for breakfast and some tempting morsels picked over from yesterday's supper of a provincial French stew. She trudged carefully through the briars and the brambles of the undergrowth, avoiding the prickly vines that brazenly crawled up the trunk of a sturdy tree.

As she searched for a spot to lay the blanket Wohali appeared, his bow and quiver of arrows upon his back, "I am back from the buffalo hunt three days. I have searched for you every day. But, you are here now. I am glad."

Lily's heart leapt as she laid eyes on Wohali. "I too have thought of you and the buffalo hunt. I am so glad you are safe."

They stood silent, then Wohali spoke. "I would like to take you to meet William. At his cabin you will see how much buffalo meat we will have for the winter.

"But, first we must eat a midday meal. I have brought you some buffalo meat and some of my mother's corn meal bread she baked fresh this morning. And, I have drawn some water from the stream that flows alongside William's cabin. It is the clearest I have ever seen even more than the clear, cool streams along the buffalo hunt."

Lily spread her blanket upon the forest floor and set out her meal, saving some of the dishes for Wohali's hard-won buffalo meat. Wohali laid out the freshly roasted meat as he spoke. "We must start for William's cabin right after our meal. It is near. But, you must be back before dark."

They ate in silence, Wohali sitting cross-legged upon the beautifully woven blanket, listening to the birds chattering to their mates or chasing a pesky stranger away from the nest, the squirrels scampering to find an acorn cache and the rabbits zigzagging along toward their burrows to fool a stealthy predator.

As they finished Lily gathered up the remains and folded up the blanket. Wohali was already untying

Gola. "We must start now if we are to be back before dark."

Lily, anxious to meet William, hastened to untie Paco, packing the dishes into her saddlebag as she mounted him. Wohali was already at her side. "I will ride slow so your pony will not tire. Gola will like the easy pace. He worked hard at the buffalo hunt. He will care for your dapple-gray. He is gentle with the newborn foals and the colts William has bred for trading."

The sun was still high as they rode for William's cabin. Unable to get through the close-knit bushy tree-tops of the Cross Timbers it lavished its rays on the prairies, much to the delight of the wildflowers that responded with the most beautiful blossoms, the reds, the yellows and the lavenders all mingled among the tall green and golden grasses that waved with the wind and tickled Paco's tail. "I must stop and gather wildflowers for William. I think they would brighten up his cabin."

Lily dismounted and handed her reins to Wohali while she bent to get the biggest blossoms she could find. Gola nuzzled Paco in a friendly gesture but he stood silent, used only to the aloof barn horses he was stabled with. Wohali reached down to steady him, clucking in a language Lily was certain only a horse could understand.

As she remounted, she bundled the flowers with a ribbon from her saddle bag and tucked them into a harness strap. They mustn't get lost or trampled on for they must be fresh for William. As she arranged herself in the saddle Wohali gazed down upon her, the sun's rays bringing highlights to her soft brown hair, her face flushed from the gentle winds wafting about with the scents of spring and her deep blue eyes almost violet the color of the prairie larkspur. Wohali thought her the most beautiful creature he had ever seen.

"We must go while the sun is still high. William will be waiting."

They rode in silence, climbing the last hill to find William hoeing the small garden he tended over the summer to harvest from its fertile soil gourds of all kinds which the Indians valued.

Wohali tied their mounts to an oak tree not far from the cabin and brought water and feed. William laid down his hoe, greeting Wohali with a raised hand, a broad grin and a look of pride he tried very hard to conceal. "Welcome, Lily. Wohali has spoken about you often. Please come in to the cabin. We will have tea and some corn meal cakes that Wohali's mother Ahyoka has shared for this special occasion. It is not often we get visitors."

Lily, awed by William's rough but attentive manner, his great height and a voice that seemed to echo from the nearby mountains, handed him the flowers without a word. "Why, thank you, Lily. What a nice surprise for an old trapper like me. We must hurry inside. They must be thirsty."

Lily followed William through the cabin door, the one room just big enough for a bed, an oak table surrounded by a few pine chairs, a cast-iron stove against the side wall, and a large oak chair with carefully carved arms and a stool in the farthest corner. A small table held a gilt-framed photograph, its image worn and fuzzy.

"There's an empty tobacco can up on the shelf there and a bucket of water in the corner. You give the flowers a drink while I boil the water for our tea."

William pulled a well-worn pot from the shelf above the stove, filled it with water from the bucket and lit the logs below. As it boiled, he took several twigs from a glass jar that had been carefully stored in the only cabinet hung on a nearby wall, its slatted pinewood doors holding a stack of chipped but serviceable crockery. "It took a lot of pelts to get the Indians to part with these Spicebush twigs. Their medicine men value them highly for what they believe are its healing powers."

"You know a lot about Indian ways."

"When I was a young buck I left the Carolinas to push west. I took a Cherokee for my wife and she was happiest staying with her people so I stayed too. Her name was Inola and I liked just watching her tidy up our sleeping corner and pounding the maize for corn bread. She could prepare small game and fresh fish the Cherokee taught me to spear so we could cook over an open fire and many a night we ate under the stars just the two of us.

She could harvest the squash, the beans and the maize with the rest of the women and turn them into the most tempting stews and soups that would please the Great Spirit himself but she was as delicate as a butterfly and as beautiful.

Then, we had a child and we named her Tayanita. She was a willful child but beautiful as Inola and as she grew Inola taught her to prepare the meal for bread and to keep our belongings tidy. I built a sapling hut and thatched it with the bark of the forest. But, though Tayanita was happy helping Inola she most wanted to run wild with the squirrels and the chipmunks."

"But, why are they not here?"

"They were killed when the Creeks raided the Cherokee. I was gone learning to hunt buffalo with the elders. When I learned of the raid I could no longer bear to stay among the Cherokee without Inola and Tayanita. I left and struck out on my own.

"I still trade with the Cherokee but I cannot live among them."

Lily's eyes strayed to the faded gilt-framed photograph that sat on the small table against the wall. A woman, dressed in ceremonial deerskin, her long dress fringed at the hem and sleeves, belted at the waist, with beads adorning the bodice and the skirt, her long braids wrapped in a beaded fabric, her headband and moccasins filled with an intricate bead design, stared out. Next to her stood a child, dressed much like the woman, but with an impish look she tried hard to hide, clutching a doll dressed very much like her.

"Now, Lily, we can set the table for our tea. If you reach up in that cupboard you will find the tea cups and some plates to set out Ahyoka's tea cakes."

At that, Wohali entered the cabin, his arms full of chopped wood. "I will lay these logs near the stove. That way they will heat the cabin and feed the burners."

Lily busied herself setting the table, the mismatched dishes chipped but serviceable. As they sat, William poured the brewed tea and set out the plate of small corn meal cakes. Before they ate, he recited a Cherokee blessing. "We thank the Great Spirit for bringing us this food and Mother Earth for nurturing the fertile soil."

Lily picked up the steaming cup. She had never tasted a brew like this and it seemed to warm her right down to her toes. She was certain she could taste the whole outdoors and the spicy aroma seemed very much like the lemon Cook often squeezed into her more exotic dishes.

The small cakes of corn meal were drizzled with honey and seemed to melt in her mouth. "Wohali, you must get Lily back very soon. The sun will go down before we know it."

"I will get the horses saddled up."

Lily gathered up the dishes but William shooed her along. "You must get going. Your folks will be worried if you don't arrive for your supper before sundown."

Wohali left to get the horses and Lily thanked William.

"I was glad to meet you, Lily. Sometime you must meet Ahyoka. She will teach you how to bead necklaces and how to turn a soft piece of doeskin into a moccasin that will take you far in the forest.

As Lily and Wohali left, the dogs snoozing by the barn awoke to chase Gola as far as they could. The sun was still high as they rode over the grassy hill.

Wohali and Lily rode quietly back to the Cross Timbers where Wohali left with the game he had bagged in the afternoon packed into his saddlebag. Lily left for home heady from the excitement of the afternoon but intent upon being on time for supper. She had promised Cook some flowers for the table and plucked the most beautiful violets and tea blossoms she could find.

The sun was lowering in the sky but the air was still fresh with the scent of spring. She sighed as Paco picked up his pace anxious to return to the stable for a brisk brush and a lump of sugar he knew Josiah the stable hand carried especially for him.

Chapter Five

I t was 1886 and Lily had just turned fifteen. It was an exciting time for Oklahoma and a change for the residents of its territory. The US government had just opened its lands to settlers from the east, pushing back further on the lands allotted the Indians. There was talk of the railroads coming in. And, settlers, not used to the rough terrain, were turning back east, unable to farm the land.

Mama and Papa were in heated discussions about the future of their daughter and her education. It was time to make some decisions and it seemed Lily was the last to be consulted.

She had spent her years in freedom, roaming the territory as she pleased, as long as she kept up with her education which came mostly from books.

Papa was now awakening her every day to accompany him to the mines. She was learning to have a business head and was responsible for much of the bookkeeping, allowing Alfred to spend more time at his plans for using the proposed railroads for shipment of corundum to be cut into ruby and sapphire gemstones and coal east and perhaps to a port for shipment to all of Europe. But, despite his enthusiasm, this she knew would take years to complete.

Lily was learning to dress in the fashions of the eighties. She favored starched shirtwaists, unadorned long skirts, low-heeled shoes with buttonhooks, and bonnets for the sun. Every now and then she added a ruffle or two and wore her hair upswept with a few ribbons or bows. But, mostly she was happiest in a woolen or leather shirt or linen for the summer, her hair held back with a large brightly colored bow along with riding breeches and the most intricately scrolled leather riding boots she could find.

As their carriage drew closer to the mines, Papa gave Lily a few last minute instructions, conferring with her on the state of their books and checking on their supplies of files, paper and auditing journals.

"Papa, when do you expect the railroads to lay track through Oklahoma?"

"I don't know, Lily. So far no company has gotten the rights to come through Oklahoma. But, when they do they will make a fortune. And, so will we. It will mean shipping our ruby and sapphire ore and coal to faraway countries.

It will also mean that we can use those profits to open new mines. Who knows what we'll discover. Oklahoma has been good to us so far. Who knows what lies beneath the mountains."

Papa never failed to look at the country around them where Lily had spent so many happy hours as a business opportunity. Although she very much wanted to please Papa she knew she could not look at the terrain about them without thinking of the many days she had spent as a lonely child nestling in the Cross Timbers among the birds and the squirrels and picking the most beautiful wildflowers of the prairies. And, especially, of the times walking among the darkest of woods to the streams where there was sunshine with Wohali since they had met and sharing their deepest secrets.

As they approached the mine Lily noticed a two-seater that signaled Jamie's arrival as well as Hector's. Hector, limping, with his arm in a sling was on the mend from a farm accident, determined to run the mines regardless. Jamie, despite Hector's stubbornness, had insisted on coming along to help.

"Good morning, Hector."

"Good morning, Miss Lily. Let me help you down."

"I can get down myself, Hector. You sit and rest."

"You know I can't do that. I have a job to do."

"Where's Jamie?"

"He's down talking to the miners and checking the veins. We're hoping for a lode soon."

At that, Lily heard the car bringing him to the top. She stared at the mine entrance as Jamie appeared, brushing the coal dust with a white linen cloth. As he stood up she was certain he had grown a foot since she saw him last.

"Well, Lily, good morning." His grin was enough to tell her he was glad to see her.

"Good morning, Jamie. What takes you away from the farm?"

"Pa needs a helper even if he is too stubborn to admit it. But, the spring planting's been done so I can be spared until the hoeing begins. I hear you're taking over the books now."

"Not quite, but I am learning. Papa can use my help every now and then and I have even thought of a new system to help speed the tallying up."

"Maybe when you're finished with the books and the men are on their own in the mine we can walk down to the piney woods. I have some cold ham and some cheese Ma got at the general store. I'm glad to share."

"I can add the leftover pot roast Cook packed and the muffins she made fresh this morning. I think we can make a nice midday meal."

As Lily headed for the station house Jamie descended once again into the mine. Lily pulled the auditing books off the shelf and filled her inkpot.

Neat rows of figures filled the books but all Lily could do was stare out the station windows into the mountains below. Flowering dogwood, black walnut and redcedar filled part of the terrain below and rocky abutments and plateaus the rest.

But to Lily none of that beauty came close to the Cross Timbers. Rough-barked stunted-growth oaks growing out of a darkened forest floor, their tight-knit leafy branches keeping away the sunlight and the sounds of a world scurrying about in wagons and run-abouts toward an uncertain future.

The visions of walks with Wohali toward the streams where sunlight filled the waters or their midday meals among the oaks with the sounds of squirrels and chipmunks scurrying about or the chirping of birds flitting through the tree branches filled her head.

"Hey, Lily, a penny for your thoughts."

Lily looked up to see a coal-dust smeared Jamie poking his head around the station house door. "Oh, Jamie, you caught me at my day-dreaming when I should have been adding up these figures. Mama says a lady doesn't daydream but pays attention to her posture and her carriage. She is certain that a young lady must watch her posture and her manners and learn witty conversation to be noticed properly in a drawing room."

"Well, you have plenty of time for that. Now I think it's time to walk the trails to the piney forest. The noon sun's high and we can set up a proper meal under the shade of the tallest tree we can find and check for pinecones. Ma can't wait 'til they drop so she can weave them into a Christmas wreath."

The sun was high as they walked the trails and Lily could feel its warmth on her back. They kicked back the pebbles as they walked, keeping score to see who could find the most. Jamie yelled into the mountains looking for an echo but the mountains did not answer back.

"Lily, Mr. Alfred says you'll be going east to a school where you'll learn all the things that will turn you into a fine lady." Jamie paused. "I think you're fine enough how you are."

"Oh, he means I'll learn needlework and how to play the piano and how to dress and make proper conversation and how to hold myself to have a good carriage. Mama says its nothing you can learn in Oklahoma but they have schools there that turn girls into fine ladies and that maybe I can marry an earl if I go abroad."

"What do earls do?"

"I don't know. I have read about noble people in some of the books Mama has sent for. They run big houses that are bigger than any you've seen here and the houses are filled with servants who do everything. I guess the earls go visiting and walk on beautiful places with beautiful gardens and take dogs that aren't like farm dogs but have servants who brush them every day. All the servants call them 'My Lord' and when they go visiting they are driven by servants in big, fancy carriages and the country ones have acres and acres of fields and people to farm them."

"Gosh, Lily, wouldn't you miss the mountains and the prairies and the piney woods?"

"I don't know. Mama says they're rich and have fancy clothes of silks and satins and they feast on food we've never seen here and they give parties all the time."

"Well, I hope you get what you want."

"That's just it. Papa would like me to stay here and take over the mines one day. But, he will do anything to please Mama."

"I guess we better just find a spot and set out our midday meal. I know we have to be back to take over before Pa decides to take over himself and set himself back from all the good Ma and I did getting him to rest."

The sun found its way through the pine trees as Jamie set down the blanket and placed the pouch of ham and cheese his Ma had packed in the middle along with some fresh-baked biscuits. He pulled out a canteen of cool spring water from a stream along his farm and Lily added the pot roast and muffins, along with china dishes and a lacy doily Mama had insisted upon.

As they ate, Lily gazed at Jamie and envied him his countenance. He had been a happy boy and now he was growing into a happy man. He loved farming and the life he had just grown into and had been expected to follow. Both his Ma and his Pa were counting on him to take over the farm and feed the little ones. His sisters were growing and even had boys they were sweet on and would marry and do the same.

But, Lily had wanted more. She wanted to see the exotic countries she had only read about and meet the kings and queens and nobles that existed in her fairy tales as well.

But, she was torn just as Mama and Papa were about her future. She was part of the land, the wildflowers she gathered in the summer among the green and yellow grasses of the prairies, the steep and unforgiving mountains with veins of ore yielding the most beautiful gemstones, and the forests with trees that stayed green all year dropping pinecones for winter wreaths and trees that bore acorns for the squirrels and brought new oak trees in the spring. And, the Cross Timbers, especially the Cross Timbers where you could hide from the world when you needed it. Where could she hide in a castle?

Jamie broke the silence. "Lily, when will you leave to go east?"

"I don't know. Mama has to make plans and Papa has to write Grandmother Paxton who I have never met. Grandmother Paxton sends a Christmas gift every year and Papa has a faded photograph of her and Grandfather Paxton when they were married on his dresser. But, the trip west to the territories has always been said to be too hard for her delicate nature and Mama has always been too busy to plan a trip east with the hardships of travel. She would rather read about faraway places than visit them. Mama likes her comforts.

"But, she makes sure Grandmother Paxton has a beautiful ruby necklace or brooch every Christmas made from the ore that Papa has pulled from the veins of the Oklahoma mountains. And, she writes beautiful letters in the script she learned from books with flourishes she inks in every now and then. And, she closes every letter with a special wax seal that stamps the family crest she sent for from Europe.

"I'll miss you, Lily. No one will be around to beat me at marbles."

"You still have your sisters. Now that they're older maybe they'll learn to beat you."

"Aw, they're busy chasing boys. That's all they talk about. I'm sure it won't be long before we see a wedding or two."

"I'll send you letters as often as I can. I'll learn a beautiful script like Mama knows and I'll tell you all about their drawing rooms and big houses and parlors and calling cards.

"I've seen their carriages in pictures and the balls they have. Ladies in beautiful gowns and gentlemen in handsome dress. They bow to each other and do elegant dances. And, they picnic on great lawns surrounded by beautiful gardens."

"When will you be back?"

"I don't know. Mama says she wants me to board at the school and stay the summer with Grandmother Paxton at her country home. Mama says Grandmother Paxton will give me a coming out ball and present me to society when I'm ready."

"Well, it sounds real elegant. I know you will have

many suitors. You're the most beautiful girl in Oklahoma."

"I'm sure you'll have a lot of girls chasing you and setting their cap for you. I'm surprised you haven't had one of those girls in town catch you already."

"I don't have time to go courting. Ma and Pa need me on the farm. And, they don't need another mouth to feed.

"We'd better get back before Pa decides to take over and break his arm all over again. We had to ride miles to get Doc Jenson and he couldn't talk any sense into Pa either."

Jamie packed up the blanket and the leftovers and handed Lily the dishes and the doily. "You'll have plenty of time to tend to the dishes in the stream out back. It looks like an easy afternoon."

As they strolled the trails toward the station house, neither in a hurry to get back, Jamie looked at the darkening sky. "We'd better hurry. It looks like it's blowing up a twister."

Jamie grabbed Lily to make a run for it, giggling as they went. They made it to the station house just as the storm came up, drenched from the heavy rains and dropped exhausted on the old, weathered pine boards of the station house floor.

Lily savored the moment, for she knew that now that Jamie was growing into his role as head of his household it would be long before he would appear at the mines again.

Chapter Six

Lily galloped across the prairies toward the Cross Timbers on the back of a beautiful red roan stallion. Paco had long since been retired to the stables but Lily made sure he had the run of the prairies he loved so much and a carrot or lump of sugar before bedtime.

Wohali had promised a visit to Ahyoka and Lily was anxious to learn the art of turning a length of doeskin into a pair of the softest moccasins which Ahyoka was very skilled at. She hastened the roan and arrived at the forest just when the sun had reached its peak and Wohali was packing up his quiver and the game he had brought down just after the sunrise had cast its hues of red and bronze, yellow and orange over the mountains, the plains and the grasslands of a vast terrain.

She tied the roan to a sturdy post oak at the edge of the woods and walked the narrow path that took her into the depths of the woods managing to step carefully along the barren forest floor to avoid the briars and tangles she was certain were out to rip the new breeches Mama had sent for. She found Wohali at the foot of a blackjack oak stroking Gola and packing up the ample bounty of small game he had managed to bag in the morning.

"Greetings, Lily. You have arrived just in time. My mother is preparing our meal so we must ride while the sun is high."

"I am ready. I have brought the fastest stallion in the stable to keep up with Gola."

"Gola is getting old but he runs like a young stallion. We have seen many good times together."

Lily stared at Wohali as he spoke. Somehow, though the woods were dark, a ray of sunshine had managed to break through the close-knit treetops and the muscles that rippled about his forearms stood out as he packed. His high cheekbones set under a mane of thick black hair glistened in the sliver of sunlight and his measured movements seemed almost to follow the aura of the antlered stags and the colorfully plumed birds she had seen so often protecting their mates and their young.

Lily knew little about young men except for what she had read in books. To her Wohali looked at this moment like all the princes and nobles she had read about all wrapped into one.

Wohali broke into her thoughts. "We must go now, Lily. I will bring Gola alongside your stallion and we will ride. Mother is anxious to see you. She has saved a length of doeskin to turn into a pair of moccasins and many beads for you to choose from."

Lily was excited to get a pair of moccasins to walk the woods in so she could peer into the nests of the robins and the chickadees and see the new hatchlings without frightening a mother robin or treading too harshly along the trails to keep the new fawns still covered with spots from romping so freely about.

Lily stopped only to gather some flowers for Ahyoka. She was a proud woman but Lily knew the blossoms would give her pleasure.

Wohali was quiet as they rode but Lily could see there was a lot on his mind. Then, he spoke. "William has drawn me into learning the skills of trading but I must keep up the farm and the hunt as the work gets harder for my mother who gets more fragile as the days go by. She took on many tasks with the loss of my father. But, she never complains."

"You have been a good son, Wohali. Your father would have been proud of you."

"My father was a proud man. He taught me a lot and my mother and I do not forget his spirit. My mother prays every day to the Divine Beings for his soul.

"She sees him everywhere. In the sun, the stars and the trees of nature. It is the Cherokee belief that his soul will remain here for as many years as he lived."

At that Lily's horse bolted at a rattler that had slunk off but had not escaped the notice of the roan. She managed to stay astride and Wohali caught the reins to slow the stallion to a halt.

The rest of the ride was uneventful and they slowed their pace to give their mounts a rest as Lily basked in the warmth of the sun's rays beaming down upon her back and admired the new blooms of the prairies as they passed.

They reached Ahyoka's cabin in time for Lily to help set out the midday meal on the small planked oaken table that held the many dishes that Ahyoka prepared from the teachings of her Cherokee elders. Four pine chairs, carefully carved, were set neatly around it.

Ahyoka's cabin was sparse but neatly kept. A faded photograph of Wohali's father dressed in deerskin breeches with two eagle feathers hanging loosely from his long dark hair adorned the dresser that was placed next to a small corner bed.

Ahyoka greeted Lily warmly and placed the wildflower bouquet in a chipped pottery vase she obviously prized. The aroma of a wonderful stew was wafting from the direction of the small wood stove along the wall.

"Lily, my son tells me you would like to learn the art of making a deerskin moccasin. I will teach you as my elders taught me. Soon you will be as quiet in the woods as Wohali and his father before him.

"Now, we must set out the bowls for our stew before it cools."

Wohali was gone to gather wood for the stove where Ahyoka turned out so many dishes. Lily could hear the dogs barking as he went. She could also hear him greeting them by name.

"You must put out the bowls my mother left to me when she went to be with the Divine Beings. I pray to our creator every day for her soul and every day those bowls are a reminder of all she taught me."

Lily reached for the three bowls Ahyoka had motioned toward and placed them carefully on the table, their signs of the sun and the moon painted on the yellow pottery a contrast to the chipped flowered dishes William had traded for some moonshine at the general store which Ahyoka also prized.

At that, Wohali came noisily into the room, carrying an armful of chopped wood, followed by a very mixed-breed grey-spotted mongrel who seemed to nip at his heels obviously trying to get his attention. As he dropped his wood on the pile by the stove he shooed the mongrel out of the cabin.

"Waya, you must be outside. You are not welcome here. You must go find food. You must be strong for we will need you to help with harvest."

The dog slunk out of the cabin but lay down outside. He was obviously more willful than the rest of the pack that ran the grounds but kept to themselves. But, he was very attentive to Ahyoka and as Wohali mentioned he would tear to pieces anyone who attacked her.

"Wohali, you must sit in the chair in the corner while Lily and I prepare the table. William has left some blocks of wood to be carved. He has gotten good trades for the totems you have pulled out of the redcedar he has left for you to whittle."

Lily finished setting up the table. She placed the pottery vase with its totems and signs of the sun and the moon in the middle. Ahyoka spooned the stew into the bowls and poured the steaming spicebush tea into cups. She placed a freshly baked corn bread on the table as well. Then, she called to Wohali. "Son, you must come and eat. You must be strong for the autumn harvest."

Ahyoka spoke to the gods and thanked them for the food they were about to eat. The aroma of the stew was hard to resist and Lily savored the tender chunks of buffalo meat that had been cooked for hours along with the corn, beans, peas and fresh tomatoes Ahyoka had harvested from the small garden she tended behind the cabin. Lily thought she had never tasted anything so wonderful as it tasted as fresh as the soft winds that crossed the prairies on a dusky summer evening.

"Lily, we must measure your feet so your moccasins fit so snugly you can walk undisturbed and as quietly as you wish. You will be one with nature as the deer and the antelope."

When they finished, Ahyoka brought out some corn meal cakes drizzled with honey and some rare syrup made from the sap of a sugar maple that stood high above the stream that ran alongside the cabin, its leaves a showy brilliant red against the autumn sky. Then, she and Lily cleared the dishes and washed them in the basin filled with the well-water Wohali had pumped when they had arrived. Wohali was anxious to get back to his carving for if he turned out many totems Ahyoka would have many stores for the winter.

Ahyoka laid out the doeskin she had tanned, a bowl of the most beautiful beads, a needle and thread, a sharp cutting tool and lengths of heavy leather to lace the moccasins with. She traced Lily's feet to the doeskin, pulled a length upward to form the sides and the flap, and let Lily cut.

Lily put the doeskin up and rubbed it along her cheeks, its softness like a feather before she cut. Then, she placed the two pieces of doeskin on the table. Ahyoka pulled a tool from the small drawer of a side cabinet.

You must make the holes as even as you can from the middle. We will lace the sides together. I will start and you will watch me. Then, you will finish and you will be ready to choose the beads."

Lily was anxious to choose the beads but she knew she must be patient. Ahyoka had already made some holes and Lily knew it was her turn. She handed Lily the small tool to punch the flap and began lacing up the sides. Before Lily knew it the moccasins were turned and she could choose the pattern.

Lily chose reds and pinks and yellows and oranges, the colors of the sunset. She chose green for the deep evergreen of the pines, and many blues for a clear sky at noon when the sun was high. Ahyoka showed her how to string the beads and make any pattern she wanted. She chose the shape of a wild lily and followed it through with her needle.

"Now you will walk softly. You will remember our day here as you walk through the soft grasses."

"Ahyoka, I will remember your kindness.

Now we must go. I have far to travel and I must be back before sundown."

Wohali led Gola and the roan from the large oak tree that had held them, watered and fed and pestered by the dogs and stray cats, back to the cabin. The sun was lowering in the sky.

Lily said her goodbyes to Ahyoka and mounted the roan. Wohali left alongside her promising Ahyoka he would return before nightfall and scolding Waya to mend his lazy ways.

As they rode toward the Cross Timbers, weary from the day but aware of the vastness of their surroundings, they spoke little, each with their own thoughts. Storm clouds were gathering overhead but neither took notice.

Chapter Seven

M ama bustled around, fixing this and that, adjusting the candlesticks that graced the large and formal cherry wood dining table they dined on every evening, making sure that every portrait of every lord and lady she had sent for from the best gallery she knew in all of Paris was straight along the walls of the parlor. "Uncle Luis and Aunt Maria will be here soon with Lita and the little ones. Everything must be perfect."

Lily was excited because Mama had given permission for Lita to stay a whole month as Lily's companion. Lily was certain they would have much to talk about. And, giggle about.

But, Mama was most interested in the large, spacious manor reflecting the elevated status she enjoyed among her brothers and sisters. She was the one who had married well and Grandmama's pride. Grandmama beamed every time she spoke of Elena. And, Elena enjoyed her position.

"Lily, would you give the dining room candlesticks to Mary to polish? They seem a little dull."

Lily could see no tarnish on the beautiful, silver candlesticks that had been a wedding present from Grandmother Paxton, but she obliged. She brought them to Mary who was new and almost her age, giving the instructions she had been charged with.

Mama then moved to the parlor where she saw dust that wasn't there and tidied up things that were already tidy.

"Lily, you must change into a more presentable outfit. Aunt Maria will think you are neglected when it comes to the fashionable garb of young ladies today."

"Yes, Mama." Lily ascended the elegant staircase with its polished brass rail and lionhead newels grateful for the opportunity to escape the frantic preparations and just wonder what Cook had dreamed up for supper. Aunt Maria and Uncle Luis and the little ones would be their guests for three days and Mama had given Cook a list of the most impressive dishes she could think of that had come from the magazines of the gentle folk of Europe taken from the best hotel chefs of the continent who were willing to share for the notoriety it brought them.

Lily took a long time assessing her large closet and the scrolled oaken dresser across from her canopied bed that held the most elegant outfits and chose a carefully tailored linen skirt with frills at the hem and a linen blouse embroidered with tiny roses and lace at the neck and the sleeves. She pulled from the finely sanded shelves along the bottom of her closet a pair of polished black leather shoes that hooked with the tiniest of pearl buttons.

Lily dressed and descended the stairs just in time to nearly be knocked over by Lita's several younger brothers and sisters. Daniel, the youngest, had grown what looked like nearly a foot and could outrun even some of the older ones. All of them rushed toward Lily, wanting the hugs she always lavished on them and begging her to play roll the hoop and touch tag. She hugged each one and then found Lita.

Lita was busy making sure her new dress which Aunt Maria had made from the finest linen was hung properly and free from wrinkles. The old buckboard Uncle Luis had purchased with money from the sale of a number of cash crops which depended on the weather had stood the test of time but was now just a rickety wagon in need of repair.

Lily hugged Lita and made sure her new dress had a special place in her own closet. Then, she helped her get settled in the lavish guest room which Mama had decorated with chairs imported from Europe in the Louis XVI style with the hope that Grandmother Paxton would one day visit.

Papa invited Uncle Luis into the parlor for a talk and a good cigar and Mama showed Aunt Maria around the gardens, newly planted with the roses that had won the latest ribbons and a variety of the pink and purple asters she loved.

Though Papa had given permission for Lily to have the run of the stable horses for Lita as well Lita preferred to leaf through the many fashion magazines that Mama had stacked in a special cabinet along with her cookbooks and the glossy magazines that featured the insides of the manor homes of the European aristocracy.

Lita marveled at the silks and satins of the duchesses' and countesses' ballgowns and the starched shirts and golden pocket watches the earls and dukes pulled from the pockets of their highly fashionable waistcoats. She swooned over the velvet loveseats that lined the ball rooms and the silk divans that were everywhere in their enormous manor houses and castles.

When Lita had her fill of devouring the magazines Lily took her for a walk around the grounds. "Come, Lita, I will show you where we picnic. Perhaps Cook will pack us a basket for our own picnics if we promise to make sure to convince Mama that Cook will have her pick of the best cooking tools that Mr. Johnson imports at the general store and maybe a gingham dress that Cook has had her eye on for months."

Lily led Lita to a natural glade of elm trees that shaded a beautifully manicured lawn with rose bushes planted at one far end and a garden of the most beautiful blue larkspur and deep purple Sweet William with small clusters of white alyssum lining the borders. The clear blue of the sky shone above and a stone bench sat in the middle.

"We must sit. No one will find us and we will have a chance to catch up on all the gossip we missed since last Thanksgiving."

Lita sat and tried to catch her breath. "Oh, Lily, everything is so beautiful. I want to marry a rich man like your Mama did. All the boys at school want to be farmers like their Pa. They'll never get anywhere. Farming is such a struggle. Every year we must cross our fingers that the pests don't get our crops. Or that there will be rain, or enough sunshine. Pa prays every year for good weather."

"But, your family seems to be doing well. Mama tells me how Uncle Luis has made a good profit with cash crops he sells in town. She says if that keeps up you might even add another room to your house or a new buggy for your horse to pull. Then, you can travel in all kinds of weather."

"Yes, Pa has an interest in the new kind of farming. He sends for bulletins all the time. But, he still worries how he is going to feed another mouth or keep Ma in the clothes he likes to see her in.

"Ma never complains. She and Pa dance in the evenings when a good crop comes in or even if there isn't one to the harmonica and the tambourine he has taught even the little ones how to play.

"But, I want more, Lily. I don't tell Ma or Pa because I don't want to hurt their feelings. They work so hard to provide for us."

"Well, maybe a rich boy will be visiting town when you and Uncle Luis go there for supplies and you can run off with him when you get a bit older. You're beautiful, Lita. He will love your dark eyes and your beautiful silky hair."

"Oh, you're so kind, Lily. But, what would any rich boy want with me? I won't be getting the education he will get and though Ma works hard to make me the nicest dresses when she can I won't have the clothes so he can show me off to his friends and family and be proud."

"Well, I think any boy would like you, rich or poor. And, if they don't you shouldn't run off with them. You wouldn't be happy. And, Cook says that being happy is the most important thing.

"Mama wants to send me east to learn the manners of a lady so I can find a rich man to marry or even to travel to Europe to marry a duke or an earl. But, I'm not sure I'd like it in Europe and I don't know anything about dukes and earls.

"Papa wants me to take over the mines when he gets on. He worries about the railroads not coming in fast enough so he can ship to Europe and keep Mama in the elegant clothes she fancies.

"But, I'm not sure what I want. Jamie knows what he wants and Wohali is sure of what he is charged to do. But, I'm not sure I will make a fancy lady who watches her posture and knows how to dress in silks and satins and says only what she has learned is proper."

"Who are Jamie and Wohali?"

"They are my friends. We will ride to the Cross Timbers and Wohali can show you how to shoot straight with a bow and arrow. And, Jamie can show you the robin's eggs and the hatchlings when they arrive."

Lita sighed. "This month will be such fun. We can do what we want with no little ones to mind and no supper to prepare.

"I wonder what it would be like to marry an earl. Then, you'd never have to prepare supper and life would be so gay. You could go to balls where the ladies were all dressed in silks and satin and the gentlemen would bow and be in velvet waistcoats with gold pocket watches and perfectly folded silk handkerchiefs in their pockets.

"I saw a gentleman once. He was in Mr. Peterson's general store and he had a perfectly pressed tweed waistcoat and he was trying to sell Mr. Peterson some bolts of silk and satin and some bonnets with ribbons and flowers all around the brims claiming they were all imported from Europe. But Mr. Peterson would have none of it. He said he had no call for the silks and satin but that the bonnets might do for church.

"After he left all the men made fun and called him a dandy. But, he was so polite and didn't chew tobacco or spit.

"I must show you the doll I made for you, Lily. She looks just like you. And, she has a silk dress. Mr. Peterson let me have the end of a bolt for no charge. He said there was nothing he could do with it anyway so I might as well have it. I made her a lace collar with the lace Ma saved from my dress she made last year and Ma showed me how to make a flounce at the bottom so she could look very grand."

"Oh, Lita. I can hardly wait to see her. I have a special chest for my dolls and a shelf that Enrico built for me to take them out when I want to and show them off."

"Ma gave me a case to bring her in. I will take her out as soon as we get back."

"We must go now. Everyone will be looking for us and Cook will probably be ready to serve supper."

As they strolled back, Lita looking around at every blossom and walking softly over the manicured lawns, they thought about the times ahead. A soft misty rain was beginning to fall, leaving moisture that seemed like morning dew on the perfect carpet of grass. They laid their plans aside in favor of enjoying the moment. After all, the future seemed so very far away.

Chapter Eight

L ily sat with Papa as they drove to the mines in their brand new buggy. The stallions the stable hands chose to hitch to it were the liveliest they could find. They stepped lively as they ascended the hills and crossed the wide prairies as they headed for the mountain that held the corundum that was made into the precious gems that adorned the wealthy and prominent folks of the east who could afford it.

Papa was looking for a big find soon to fit in with the schedule of the railways all vying to lay tracks through Oklahoma and on farther west. Carrying the ore east to be turned into precious gems and perhaps to be set in the most intricate and fashionable jewelry of the times or shipped to Europe to be fashioned by royal designers would be more profitable for Papa than ever before.

Lily knew Jamie would be at the mines on this day and she made sure to go in with Papa. Papa had asked Hector to spare Jamie from his farming duties for this one day so he could lead the miners to the sections of the mine that he thought held the most promise of a wide lode that would bring the most profit. Papa said that Jamie had a natural instinct that led him to the best spots in a mine like a homing pigeon or a dowser running into a natural geyser.

"Lily are you up on your book work?"

"Yes, Papa. I have kept it up. I can almost run the books by myself."

"I'm glad. We've been in the black for some time now and your new system helps to tally it all up faster. I wouldn't be surprised if you could run the accounts by yourself someday and even the mines themselves."

"I'm sure I could, Papa. Then you could take it easier and you and Mama could travel a bit and even take in some of those shows that travel west and bring all the acts from the east just like those rich people have performing for them at theaters with velvet curtains and chandeliers or even in the parlors of their mansions."

"But, Mama wants you to go east to boarding school to learn the arts of fine ladies. Here you can only look at them in books. I think Mama is right to want a more refined life for you, Lily. Oklahoma is a rough territory and not the place for a refined young lady."

"Papa you have given me everything you know how. I have learned a lot that girls in the east have never been taught. But, I will do as Mama says. I know she wants the best for me."

The stallions slowed down as they reached the mountain and labored up the steep ascent navigating the paths with a little more difficulty carefully and gracefully avoiding the elms and the maples and the redcedars that stood in their way.

As they reached the station house, Hector patted the horses and took the reins.

"Mornin' Mr. P. Mornin', Miss Lily. I trust you had a good ride in that new buggy of yours? It ought to take the hills a lot better than the last one."

"It does, Hector. There's twice as much padding in these seats as the last one. It's made by a company in Philadelphia that ships west by the rails. Soon they'll be able to ship all the way to Oklahoma when the railways get the okay from the federal government.

"But for now they can get them pretty close and Enrico and a stable hand can pick them up with a lot less trouble than before the track was laid. I'm hoping for an answer soon on when the tracks will go through Oklahoma. We'll all do pretty well when that happens,

Hector. You can get the missus some fancy new clothes and add another room for those little ones."

"We're doing alright now that Jamie has taken over. He has all these new ideas about cash crops and maybe selling in town."

"He's a good boy, Hector. You did right in raising him."

"Well, he's here today like you asked, Mr. P. I hope he can find us some lodes that'll bring us a lot of ore."

Lily ignored the talk about Jamie. She just wanted to find him to see if he would walk the piney woods with her. She was anxious to check the pinecones to see if they would be ready to drop on time for a fall gathering.

"Jamie is down in the mines now, Miss Lily. But, he'll be back up soon and I'll tell him you're here."

"Thank you, Hector. I'll be in the station house looking over the books."

Lily knew Papa was waiting to get a report from Hector so she hurried into the station house. She knew Papa would rather be down in the mines with the men like he had been as a young prospector but she also knew it took all of his time balancing the books, overseeing the shipping, and planning for the future.

She also knew he was keeping his eye out for claim jumpers because the more settlers drifting into the territories, the more there were prospectors looking for an easy way out.

Lily filled the inkpots and straightened up the piles of papers laying carelessly around the station house. She then set to work to check over the books, neatly tallied in binders kept in the locked cabinets along the wall. Sent for from the east, they hardly had the hand-hewn look of the cherry wood, redcedar or oaken cabinets of their manor house but they had served Papa well over the years.

As she worked she wondered about Wohali and the responsibilities he already had. William was getting on and she knew he would be asked to help out and perhaps take over the trading business that William had already established. But she wasn't certain that was what Wohali wanted. The son of a father who had been run off from his own tribe he would not be welcome in any Cherokee clan or any tribe friendly to the Cherokee who chose to make war instead of treaties with the new federal government.

Jamie was the only one she knew who was happy with his lot. A happy boy, he had grown into a happy man. She envied him, but was happy he paid attention to her. Without brothers or sisters Lily was without playmates on a regular basis and had learned a lot from Jamie who had been patient enough to teach her.

As she mused Jamie poked his head into the station house. "Lily, are you ready to walk the woods? Pa told me you'd be here and we have lots of time to spend. The men are headed in a whole new direction and it looks real promising. I hope we can beat the new settlers moving in before their time. There's a whole lot of them coming ahead of the government opening up the territory to new settlers."

"I think Papa is ahead of them. He has good markets he has found through the years and he is trying to open new ones with his ties to the railroads. He knows the mines better than any settler."

"I think you're right. Mr. P. has a good head on his shoulders. The miners are lucky to have him.

"So pack up and get ready to walk. Ma packed a good mid-day meal for both of us."

Lily took her pouch with Cook's leftover French chicken casserole to add to the goodies Jamie's Ma always took the time to provide. She was glad for his generosity but knew he needed a lot to fill up his tall frame. And, she knew he worked hard on the farm.

As they strolled the path toward the piney woods, Jamie slowed his gait to match hers. "Papa is glad you could take time out of the farming to help out here at the mine. He thinks a lot of your work."

"There's plenty of work to do on the farm but the weather's helped out this season. We've been lucky. Enough sun and rain and the pests don't come 'til later. I've even had time to help Ma figure out Abby's wedding. And, Samantha's next. She has a boy sweet on her and they're planning to get married next spring."

"Sounds like you're busy. Soon you'll have lots of nieces and nephews running around."

"Well, lots of work before that. Abby's marrying a boy whose family is pretty well off. They're giving them an acre of land on their own farm to start with. So, he's planning to build a cabin before they tie the knot. And, he'll need plenty of help. So, I guess my time will be pretty well taken up.

"But, Samantha and her sweetheart are different. He lives in town and he has a job at the general store delivering goods. But, it doesn't pay much. And, his family lost everything last year so they can't help out. I tried to interest him in farming but he doesn't know the first thing about it. And, he holds no interest. He says he's a townie and that's that. So, Ma is trying to get them to wait.

"Ma says we can't have another mouth to feed and when the little ones start coming she has no room. I'm trying to turn some of our fields into cash crops but that will take a year or two. Mr. Anderson at the general store in the town near us says he'll take all we can grow. He says the town folks don't have enough room to grow much.

"Some of the crops he asks for we have never grown. I have to find out how to grow what they want before I can plant any of it. But, I'm set on doing it. I've sent for some bulletins on growing seasons in the territories. I think I'll be able to send for the seed and start the planting next year."

Lily had always looked up to Jamie. He knew what he wanted and he went after it. "Will we be able to check the pinecones to see if they'll be ready for fall gathering?"

"Of course. And, we'll make sure we find time in the fall to gather the best ones."

They reached the woods just as the sun started lowering in the sky. Jamie found the perfect pine tree to spread the blanket under its shade. He pulled some wonderful cheese and bread his Ma had freshly baked from his pack and added some perfectly salted ham to the plates Lily set out. He had drawn water from the well outside the mine and had some fresh baked cookies to set out along with it.

Lily wondered how she would ever get along in the east without Jamie there to be the big brother, the one with the knowledge of the forests and the birds that live in them, the waters that run through them and how they can be used to water the crops. The thirst for learning, the desire only to care for a family he cared so much for.

She looked over at the pine trees, their majestic presence a comfort even in the winter when they stayed staunchly green, a reminder that even when other trees laid down their leaves to rest their weary boughs spring would be on its way once again and the sun would shine over plowed fields and the birds would sing and the prairies would once again be filled with the early blossoms of wildflowers and the sun would preside over it all.

Lily gazed at Jamie, his joy evident in the meal set out before him provided mostly by the pigs he raised, the cow that grazed on the grasses around their rough-hewn cabin, and the crops he labored over at planting time.

She decided not to disturb him until he finished. The pinecones and the mine's books could wait. The only sounds she heard were the squirrels and the chipmunks scampering about and the birds minding their young ones.

Chapter Nine

L ily headed for the Cross Timbers on the back of a young frisky stallion. His neatly brushed chestnut coat glistened in the sunlight and his flaxen mane flew with the wind.

Her sixteenth birthday had come and gone and Mama was still basking in its glow. She had spared no expense and all her relatives had come from near and far. Grandmama Manuela had come with many combs in her hair ready to dance the night away to the beat of a tambourine.

Cook had baked a cake with more layers than Lily had ever seen, the house burst with streamers and the gardens were lit with lanterns so bright they competed with the starlight.

Wohali had been away on the annual buffalo hunt and Lily was anxious to see how he had made out and how much meat Ahyoka would have to salt and store away. When she reached the Cross Timbers she tied the stallion to the sturdiest post oak she could find, donned her moccasins and carefully trod the path that led to Wohali's favorite spot, avoiding the tangles and the briars that would surely tear at her clothing despite the darkness of the forest.

She found Wohali packing up the game he had bagged and patting Gola at the same time. As soon as he saw Lily he spoke. "I have waited for you to come. We brought down much buffalo at the hunt and I have brought some jerky for you to taste. We will have many provisions for the winter.

Lily looked at Wohali. He had grown from a boy into a man before her eyes but she had not noticed before. His long black hair framed a face of high cheek bones beneath eyes of limitless depth. His frame, now filled out, had the strength of the Greek gods she had only read about.

Lily spread a blanket and Wohali pulled the buffalo jerky from his pack and laid it out. She added a slice of her birthday cake she had saved and a hearty serving of the slow-cooked beef stew Cook had labored over the night before.

"William has asked me to keep his horses for him. He is getting on and would like me to learn the ways of trade. It will take me long to make a good horse trade so he will start me out with the trades of my wood carvings and many of the crops that the tribes don't grow."

"You will do well,. You are wise and patient."

"My mother gets more fragile every day and I must care for us both. But, she still goes into the fields and pounds the corn meal and lights the fires to warm our stews and bake our bread."

"You have honored your father's request and cared for your mother. Your father would be proud."

"His spirit still is with us. I know he watches over us."

Wohali reached into his pack as he spoke. "I have made you a gift. It is a totem of a bear. The Cherokee believe the bear is a symbol of courage. It will keep you safe."

Lily ran her hands over the smooth oaken circle, so carefully sanded, a black bear nestled in the middle. "I will keep it always."

Wohali was silent as he finished the remains of the meal. Then he rose. "We must walk along the stream. There I will look for the speckled trout."

Lily packed up the dishes and folded the blanket, neatly storing it in her pouch. Then she stood, following Wohali as he led her through the dark woods, grasping her hand to keep her from the tangles and briars that wove their way around the trunks of the sturdy post and blackjack oaks that played host to some of the worst thorny plants that crept into the forest.

As they reached the grassy plain bathed in sunlight, they walked along the banks of the stream, its waters sparkling and clear. "We must walk upstream where the fish gather. There we will find the biggest meal."

Wohali reached for her hand to keep her on the path where the stream narrowed and the bank became a steep ravine. As they walked neither spoke, hushed by new feelings rising within them.

As the stream widened and the banks became less steep Wohali stopped. "We can rest here and I will wade the waters to find a fat fish for an evening meal. You must hold my pouch to keep it safe."

Wohali left his shirt on the grasses that covered the bank and waded into the middle of the waters now rushing downstream. His arm muscles honed on the buffalo hunt and the difficult labor of plowing and planting in earth so often infertile glistened in the sunlight.

The speckled trout were plentiful and Wohali bagged two with almost little effort, his hands clasping them tightly as he climbed the bank grasping the slippery fish and getting them into the pouch.

"I must leave for the east. Mama is sending me to a boarding school where I will learn the manners of the rich."

"By Cherokee beliefs I am old enough to take a woman. But, the only woman I have ever wanted was you.

"I know we must part. William has said that the Cherokee cannot get in the way of the white man's desires."

Wohali packed up and took Lily's hands in his. "You will always be with me. In the hunt of the woods and in the stars we have seen together so many times as the moon rises in the sky.

"Do not forget where you come from. You are a part of these hills as the trees that have clung to the earth that nourishes them."

They walked back, each lost in their own thoughts, facing the future with as much strength as they each could muster.

Wohali untied Gola and brought him alongside her stallion. As they parted she mounted her horse as Wohali rode off toward Ahyoka's cabin. She watched as he disappeared in the distance.

She would slow the stallion down so she could savor the prairies and the wildflowers. The mountains loomed in the distance as dusk settled over the prairie and the mountains took on a purple hue as the pinks and the reds of the sunset rose over them.

The prairies looked more beautiful than ever bathed in the rosy glow of a setting sun. She hurried the stallion. She had promised Mama to be back before sundown.

Chapter Ten

L ily looked around to see if she had packed every garment she could fit into the heavy trunks Mama had ordered to hold her wardrobe. She would try to find a corner to fit at least two of her dolls. Despite her status on the threshold of the adult world she was not certain they could be left behind.

It had been decided that Lita would accompany her as a companion. Mama offered to pay all expenses and Aunt Maria was happy that Lita would have an education that she and Uncle Luis could never give her but she would miss her eldest daughter and would have to enlist the next oldest to help with the care of the little ones and fulfill the many chores it took to run a household.

Lita was excited that she would rid herself of the rough ways of the frontier and learn the fine art of the eastern drawing room. She was certain she would find a young man who would elevate her status and she would be the envy of all the girls in town who had dresses made of the latest bolts that Mr. Peterson had brought in from the east and laughed at her simple homespun.

Lita was expected to arrive soon with Uncle Luis who had been asked to stay for supper and the night. Cook had prepared a special send-off meal that consisted of several courses and the best French dishes she knew how to prepare.

As Lily put the last dress she had decided to take in the trunk with the others she heard the clatter of the buckboard below. She ran down the stairs as Lita entered.

"Oh, cousin, I'm so glad you're here."

Lita seemed quieter than usual. "Oh, Lily, we will be so far from home. Ma packed us some sausages and cheese and some bread baked with the wheat Pa put in this year."

"That sounds like just what you young ladies will need," said Mama as she beamed upon them both. "Now, Lita, why don't you come in and Josiah will bring your things in. We have gotten a trunk for you too so we will make sure your clothes are pressed and laid out so they'll be fresh when you need them."

"Oh, thank you Aunt Elena. Mama made me two dresses, one gingham and a linen she spun herself."

"They sound just beautiful. I'm sure you will look very grand in them." Mama disappeared toward the kitchen as she spoke. "Lily, you can show Lita to the guest room while I check on Cook. I see Papa has gone out to help Uncle Luis with the buckboard."

Lily put her arms around Lita. "I'm so glad you'll be with me. I don't know what I'd do if you didn't come. I know we'll find so many things to do. They have all kinds of shows and shops in the east. Papa says there is no general store but there are shops with just dresses in them and even barber shops for men."

Lita's dark eyes widened as she listened to the tales of a place she had never heard of. Lily filled her in with all she knew but that was very limited. Papa never spoke about where he came from or why he left. Grandmother Paxton was a woman of few words even in her letters.

Josiah took Lita's bags, sturdy sacks of burlap with handles of hemp Aunt Maria had spun into flax from the new plants Uncle Luis had just put in with an eye to talking Mr. Peterson into selling the hemp back east to the shipyards to turn into sails and rope that would take the brutal lashings of the winds and the rains of the sea. Mary came in and took them in for ironing and folding and laying into the new trunk Mama had purchased for Lita.

"Oh, cousin, I am not used to such attention. I hope I will fit into the ways of a school I know nothing about. I hope I will not shame you by my awkwardness."

"You could never shame me, Lita. You are the most beautiful girl I know. And, the most thoughtful. We will learn together."

At that Mary came in to summon them for supper. They slipped downstairs arm in arm, carefully and attentively navigating the large, circular staircase, its brass lionhead newels polished to a shine, and headed for the elegantly appointed dining room.

The talk, of course, was about their journey and what they would see. Mama talked about Boston where Grandmother Paxton had put down roots as if she had been there herself. Papa kept to himself, quiet though he had grown up there and knew the most first-hand.

Mama was proud of her knowledge and had seen photographs of the city from time to time in books she had sent for. She especially wanted Grandmother Paxton to think her son had married somebody learned since she knew her lineage was no secret and Grandmother Paxton had not hidden her displeasure at the marriage.

Mama also wanted to be the big sister to Uncle Luis and the favored daughter of Grandmama. She knew Uncle Luis looked up to her and she didn't want to lose her standing or disappoint. She spoke expansively about the city though her visits were from books.

"Lily, you will see big buildings you have never seen before. And, so many people. All in one place. And, they will be hurrying to attend an opera or a formal music performance with music we can only read about. And, the government buildings. All made of brick."

"What do you think, Papa. What was it like when you were there?"

"It was like a village and my early years were spent on a small farm at the edge of town. But, when Grandfather figured out how to turn a loom by the power of water he built a brick building down by the Charles River and turned it into one of the first factories in Boston. He was able to ship bolts and bolts of fabric to Europe right out of the Boston harbor and we became rich. He built a big house on a hill overlooking the city and Grandmother was accepted into the highest society and claimed ancestry as far back as the Pilgrims.

"Grandfather expected me to take over the factory but I wanted to strike out on my own. I left as a young man to prospect in the territories and settled here."

Mama rang for dessert. Cook had outdone herself with a beautiful cherry cobbler served on a Limoges porcelain platter.

After murmurs of appreciation for Cook everyone rose. Papa to retire to the parlor with Uncle Luis for some business and politics talk, a good cigar, and perhaps a glass of brandy and some cards.

Mama left for the kitchen and Lily decided she and Lita would walk the grounds for some good gossip and some plans for the future. The night air was chilly and lanterns lit the gardens as they strolled.

Lita looked carefully around, the roses bathed in moonlight, every blade of grass a uniform height. "Someday I may have something like this. But, I'm not sure what the little ones will do without me. They hide behind my skirts when they've done some mischief or skipped a chore which they know I'll do without telling."

"They will not forget you, Lita, or all that you have taught them."

"I hope Pa will get enough from his new crops so they will be able to go to school in town. Ma tries to find time to teach them but she has so many chores the sun goes down often before she has time to tend to their lessons."

"I overheard your Pa telling Papa he has high hopes for the hemp he put in. He says if the railroads get permission to go through the Oklahoma territories he can ship directly east. Papa has an interest in the railways but not much influence. He is waiting for them to lay rails near enough to the mine so he can send ore east or even overseas to be turned into gemstones without the time it takes to get them to the depots already built."

"Lily, you know so much about the mines. I know nothing about farming except for my chores."

"Your Pa wants you to have a life of ease and not struggle like he and your Ma. He is sacrificing to let you go. Every hand counts on a farm."

"I hope I will make Ma and Pa proud."

"I know you will Lita. You have worked hard."

Lily looked around. She decided to keep her own thoughts to herself. Lita needed her strength.

As she looked around she thought of Wohali. She wished for him success at learning the skill of the trade. But, as she looked above her, not one star twinkling though she searched the expanse of the sky, eerie in its stillness, she was certain that although the city of Boston was said to be populated with 300,000 citizens, without their meetings exploring the Cross Timbers or sharing a meal on its darkened floor, or riding the prairies with the sun at their backs, she would be very much alone.

Chapter Eleven

L ily looked out the window of her room at Miss Stanton's School for Girls and marveled at the passers-by as they strolled in their fashionable outfits of hats and gloves and long ruffled skirts for the ladies and top hats and vests and pocket watches for the gentlemen.

Boston was as proper and bustling as anything she had ever seen. The city was as refined and cultured as the Oklahoma territories were rough and tumble.

Lily was not certain that she could ever come up to the model of the ladies she saw strolling along the cobblestone walks below but she was willing to try. She read all the books Miss Stanton had required of her students and practiced her posture and her gait as best she could.

Meals at Miss Stanton's school were formal and tea was served promptly at four. Tiny finger sandwiches on crustless lightly buttered white bread filled with thinly sliced cucumber and tinned salmon shared space on highly polished silver trays with scones and the thickest strawberry preserves and tiny tea cakes.

Except for the servants men were allowed into the building only as chaperoned guests in the parlor or as a student's guest for dinner. Miss Stanton entertained in her own private quarters but was in attendance in the dining hall at every meal in her position as headmistress.

Lita peeked her head in as Lily mused. "Cousin, we must hurry. We mustn't be late for the first meal of the day."

Lily picked up the floral fringed shawl she had laid on a Louis XIV chair, its clawed feet turned in an ivory wood, that faced her dressing table and draped it across her shoulders over a white linen shirtwaist embroidered with tiny red roses tucked into a dark silk poplin skirt and hugged Lita. "Did you sleep well?"

"I did. I have received much news from home. Pa is expecting a good crop this year and Ma is planning another room so the little ones don't have to sleep all in one bed. She is knitting me a scarf for the long cold winter and is making it in my favorite color blue. She claims she won't know me when I return since I wrote her I will be learning piano and harp and studying French."

"Mama is so excited that I will be studying French. She thinks by the time we leave here I will be ready to travel to Europe and entice a French count to marry me."

"Well, we are learning the waltz. And, the Gavotte is on the schedule. You will be well prepared."

"I'm not sure I will be wanting to spend my days planning balls and ordering servants around but I will do my best to learn the social graces. I do miss the days I spent with Papa at the mines. Mama says it's getting closer to the railroads laying track through Oklahoma so Papa is working longer days to get more out of the mines and stockpiling the ore to have it ready when Oklahoma rails connect to the Missouri depot. I'm sure he would be surprised to see the ships leaving the Boston harbor crammed with the goods of the local merchants and would like to have the raw corundum on one of those steamers."

"Miss Stanton says it's best to leave business to men. I hardly know what Pa goes through. But, I wouldn't mind overseeing an estate. I would plan balls and fine parties and spend the days in fine carriages visiting wealthy matrons in the drawing rooms of their big stone mansions to discuss the latest gossip and scandals."

As they reached the dining hall they stopped their chatter and entered as gracefully as they could. They seated themselves at a small mahogany wood table with pineapples carefully carved along the elegantly scrolled legs, already set up with delicately embossed silver egg cups and plates of biscuits and slightly iced fruit dainties and began to chat. Servants poured seasonal freshly squeezed orange juice into crystal goblets and coffee from embossed silver coffee urns into delicate bone china cups, a beverage made popular by the protests of the Boston tea party.

As they sat, they noticed the girls at the other tables chatting demurely. One of them dressed in a lovely frock of blue with flounced skirt and wristlets approached their table. "You girls are new. It's lovely to meet you. My name is Pricilla Taylor. I'm Prissy to my friends. I hope you will like it here."

"I'm sure we will. My name is Lily and this is my cousin Lita."

"Welcome to you both. I'm from Boston but many of the girls are from much farther away. Where are you from?"

"We are from the Oklahoma territories."

"You have come a long distance. Indian country. I thought everyone was Indian in the territories."

"There are some who have left the east to prospect or seek their fortune. My Papa grew up right here in Boston."

"Miss Stanton has added geography to our studies. But, much of it is not well known. She said girls may study the many disciplines but they must not speak about them when in the company of men. It is a lady's job to let the gentleman shine when it comes to knowledge and to be only a helpmeet to him throughout courtship and marriage.

"We must get together some time. There is a lot to see in Boston and I would be glad to show you parts of it the tourists never see. Perhaps you could visit my home for Sunday dinner. I'm sure Mama and Papa would be glad to meet you."

"That is a very kind invitation. I hope we can repay you sometime. My grandmother lives in a home on Beacon Hill. I'm sure you will be welcome there as well."

Prissy's perfect coiffure and the cascade of beautiful light brown curls that hung beneath the nape of her neck held by combs of delicate shell and pearls that glistened in the rays of the sun attempting to peek through the rather dismal many-paned long windows that lined the wall of the dining hall belied her nature but her impish grin and the dimples she flashed so often gave it away.

"I must go now and attend to my studies. But, please visit my room when you have a moment. I can let you in on all the school gossip and scandals swirling about Boston."

Prissy left the dining room as swiftly as she had approached their table. Both Lita and Lily were as silent as if an Oklahoma twister had hit without warning. Lily spoke first. "We must select our iced dainties and finish our eggs. We have studying to do to catch up with the other students."

"I'm not sure I can make you proud, cousin. The girls here have grown up with servants and no hard work. They don't know what it's like to labor in the fields before dawn and hope nature favors the crops you have worked so hard to sow."

"We will work together. We will sit and converse as if we were in the finest parlor in all of Europe and we were surrounded by lords and ladies in their most beautiful finery of velvets and silks and fancy waistcoats and pocket watches of gold and inlaid rubies and diamonds."

"I will work as hard as I can. I do not want to disappoint Ma or Aunt Elena."

"I know you will not disappoint them. As much as your Ma wants you to have what you want I know she misses you and would be happy to have you back minding the little ones and helping your Pa sow the first seeds of spring."

As they walked back arm in arm, strolling slowly through the corridors of the staid old brick mansion that Miss Stanton had turned into a school for girls they marveled at the stone sculptures lining the walls, most of them Greek gods or antiquities of an indescribable nature. Lily longed to sculpt them but Mama had deemed artwork too messy for their carefully tended manse.

As they parted, they vowed to study more frequently and listen more carefully in class. Lily opened the door to her sparse but well-appointed room. She studied the garments hanging in the ample closet so she could make an impression on Miss Stanton for afternoon tea.

Chapter Twelve

L ily searched her wardrobe for the proper outfit to wear to Grandmother Paxton's. Mama had instructed her to wear her very best and be mindful of her manners and her speech.

She chose a fashionable deep green silk with lovely flounces and a bit of lace with a matching parasol in case they strolled the gardens and a pair of elegant highly polished black leather shoes with a slight heel that showed off a multi-looped bow at the toe. She dressed her hair in little ringlets along the sides and across her forehead and held the rest with studded tortoise shell combs and dabs of strongly scented pomade.

Grandmother was sending her carriage over to bring her to her home on Beacon Hill for a weekend stay and Lily was anxious to make a good impression. She carefully packed a supply of her very best grooming aids, an extra day outfit and linen nightclothes in a brocade satchel and went down the plain wooden staircase to Miss Stanton's office.

Lily knocked softly on the office door although she could see Miss Stanton bent over her desk engrossed in a large set of books and figures. "Please enter."

Miss Stanton looked up pleasantly, but it was plain to see that she was reluctant to lose her concentration on what was obviously a serious task. "Come in, Lily. It's nice to see you stirring about on such a pleasant day. We encourage our girls to take advantage of the weekend sunshine and perhaps take a stroll in the fresh air about us. Our gardens out back have been carefully tended and the asters should be in bloom about now."

"Thank you, Miss Stanton. But, I came to get permission to leave for the weekend. I believe Grandmother Paxton sent a note explaining her invitation and that I would be brought back following our visit in the evening just slightly after sundown."

"Yes. I received her request. I will notify George to be on the lookout so he can let you in as soon as you arrive.

"Please tell your grandmother how much we appreciate her charitable donation to the library. We have been able to purchase many newer editions of our etiquette collection as well as a number of other textbooks in disciplines we are just beginning to teach. It has been suggested we add math and science to our curriculum along with the geography we just began last year. They will be helpful in running a household and overseeing the gardens as well. And, geography will add to the enjoyment of world travel.

"I'm especially pleased to have purchased many new editions of piano etudes and others for the study of the harp."

"I will tell Grandmother. I know she thinks very highly of your school. It was at her insistence that Mama and Papa were encouraged to enroll me here."

"Well, I'm glad it worked out. You have been a very reliable student and a pleasant young lady to have around. I hope you will absorb as much as you can while you are here.

"You are welcome to wait in the parlor until your carriage arrives. George will fetch you when it is time."

"Thank you Miss Stanton."

Lily looked around at the almost empty parlor and seated herself at the far end. One girl had a gentleman caller but they were talking in low tones sitting in two high-backed chairs discreetly nestled in the corner. Every now and then the girl giggled.

As Lily mused on the progress she and Lita had made in the etiquette of manners and gait George leaned his head in and announced that her carriage had arrived. He took her satchel and led her to a small but plushily appointed carriage with the Paxton family crest and the name of Grandmother's mansion stenciled in gold triumphantly on the side. The coachman wore a livery of scarlet coat embroidered with gold braid, held with gold buttons and stitched with the family crest above black knee breeches and long white stockings.

George handed her satchel to the coachman and helped her into the carriage. "Now, you mind to wait for me when you arrive back. I'll help you down and take your bundles."

"I'll remember, George. Thank you."

"Now you have a good visit, Miss Lily."

The carriage drove off without a hitch. Lily settled herself against the plush purple velvet of the seat held by a series of velvet buttons carefully placed and arranged her petticoats and the green silk. It wouldn't do to arrive with a wrinkle.

Boston passed before her eyes as she gazed out of the window. Posh sections of great office and government buildings and large department stores with men in dark suits and hats and women in fine dress with hats and gloves followed by servants scurrying about the cobblestone walks. Then, as swiftly as they had come they vanished and were replaced by rutted dirt roadways lined with ninety-nine cent stores, small groceries and markets with hatless men ambling about the walkways in open loosely hanging unmatched jackets, butchers standing outside with stained aprons and hats and women with plain cotton shirtwaists and long dark skirts, an apron tied about their waist.

As they climbed the hill to Grandmother's home Lily saw a river below, tall stately brick row houses with long narrow windows, wrought iron railings, and window boxes filled with the most beautiful well-tended flowers sitting above narrow brick walkways and cobbled streets, and lit with the most elegant gaslights at dusk. Lily began to feel an anxiety she tried to suppress.

The rest of Beacon Hill was filled with the estates of the wealthy. Grandmother's sat at the very top with a beautiful view of the Charles River below and the Boston skyline in the hazy distance. The carriage pulled neatly onto the cobblestone circle and a servant rushed out to help Lily as she stepped daintily out of the carriage, mindful of her petticoats and the hem of her green silk dress which she lifted ever so slightly to keep the dust raised by the carriage from soiling it.

"Welcome to Haversford House, Miss Lily. My name is Elias and I will oblige you with anything you need that your maid Anna cannot provide. Just ring for me if there is anything I can do for you.

"Mrs. Paxton is waiting in the library to greet you. Follow me and I will see to it that Anna takes your satchel to the green room where you will be staying. Mrs. Paxton has ordered tea in honor of your arrival."

The library was furnished in plush leather with an exotic oriental carpet as its focal point. Volumes and volumes of books on adventure, travel and history to informative books on science and the best novels of the century lined the walls. Grandmother sat on a plush loveseat with a silver tea service laid out before her on a mahogany table with elegantly sculpted legs.

Lily decided to enter with the best composure she could muster. Grandmother looked foreboding but she remembered Mama's words.

"Good evening, Grandmother. It was kind of you to extend an invitation for the weekend and send for me. I have been anxious to meet you."

"And, I you, Lily. You are all I have of my Alfred. How is your Papa?

"He is fine, Grandmother. He sends his best and hopes you are fine too."

"Now come closer child and let me look you over. My eyesight isn't what it used to be."

Lily stepped forward gingerly, mindful of her petticoats and her gait. Grandmother took her in with a very exacting eye. "Now sit down and we will have some tea before it gets cold."

Lily was careful to take lemon with the beautiful silver tongs set on the small silver tray and take only one scone. Ladies must never imbibe or eat heartily lest it expand their figure to proportions unsuitable to gentlemen.

"Now tell me, child. How was your journey east?"

"My cousin and companion Carmelita and I traveled by train from the Missouri depot where Papa and Enrico had taken us in Papa's new carriage. We had sleeping and dining arranged for us and porters to help with our every need."

"Yes, I have heard of this train travel. My friends have not indulged so I have little knowledge of its amenities. But, I understand it is far preferable to the vagaries of traveling by coach with its many inconveniences and the length of time it takes to reach a destination.

"My friends prefer to travel abroad and of course steamship travel is filled with luxury if you have a strong constitution. Saltwater air revives the spirit and land travel even by train is filled with dust and the soot of the new steam engines.

"Now, Lily, how have you taken to Miss Stanton's school?"

"I have learned a lot and Miss Stanton expects a lot of us. She wanted to make sure I thanked you for your generous donation to the library. She has been able to purchase many new books."

"Elizabeth Stanton is a lovely and courageous woman. She lost her fiancé in the war. He was a dashing officer who distinguished himself in battle.

She decided in her grief to open a school for girls so they would have the same opportunities she had to find a husband worthy of her accomplishments and plan a useful life of contribution as a helpmeet to an important man and a life of charity to those less fortunate.

"It's surprising what trouble the powerful of Boston caused her in her quest because she had no man involved in her endeavor. They conspired to keep her from being able to move in anywhere. But, she persisted and one anonymous gentleman who held a lot of sway over the elite quietly backed her and she has built the school into one of the best in the country.

"Now, finish your tea and we will get you settled. I will ring for Anna."

As Lily followed Anna up the grand staircase she was aware of the grandiosity of her surroundings but too weary to take stock. Portraits of ancestors lined the walls and Chinese vases were everywhere.

The green room was magnificent by any standards. An oriental carpet lay across the highly polished oakwood floors and the four-poster bed had a beautiful floral canopy that matched the heavy drapes pulled back beside the heavy leaded-glass windows, some panes elegantly patterned, some clear.

"I hope you will be comfortable here, Miss. I will help you into your night clothes when you are ready. Madam has requested a light supper be sent to your room so that you might rest and refresh yourself for the morrow. I'm sure she has plenty of activities planned and you will meet the other guests.

"Thank you, Anna. I will be fine."

As Anna left her for the evening Lily settled herself in the plushily covered green-silk armchair in the corner with the cherrywood footstool covered in matching silk embroidered with a large rose surrounded by tiny florets of lilacs. She slipped into the green silk slippers Grandmother had thoughtfully provided.

As she headed for the four poster giving in to the weariness of the day, she pulled back the drapes of a window and peered out of a small clear pane. The stars seemed to be standing still in a darkened sky and she could see the skyline of Boston all lit up.

She thought of Wohali and the many times they had made a wish together on a shooting star that had dashed across the sky, its destination unknown but its determination apparent. She climbed up on the feather bed and lay down on the silken sheets, comforters

118

piled upon her. She must sleep for tomorrow would be a busy day.

Chapter Thirteen

L ily rose with the dawn although the room remained darkened until Anna appeared and pulled back the drapes letting the considerable light of the day in. A light breakfast was scheduled in the breakfast chamber so the weekend guests could get acquainted and plan the day's activities.

Lily chose a plain blue linen with flounced hem and wristlets and lace and embroidery adorning the collar and cuffs. She added a golden cuff bracelet inlaid with tiny diamonds and emeralds and a brooch of shell pearls in varied hues. Her footwear was simple. Tanned leather boots laced up and polished to a shine.

Anna helped her dress and coifed her hair in a simpler style than she had arrived in. It was held back with wispy strands to the side and a cascade of curls forming the rest. The young maid added a few daubs of highly perfumed pomade and pinched Lily's cheeks to bring them to a delicate and ruddy red.

"Now, Miss, you are ready and if I must say look lovely. Much rested since your arrival."

"Thank you, Anna. Do you know how many other guests have arrived?"

"Madam usually likes a houseful. She claims it is more amusing that way. But, this weekend she has kept it to a smaller number. I believe there will be young master Edmond and his mother who was involved in a scandal a number of years ago and lost her husband to a younger woman. But, she has maintained her wealth and her reputation and is very much sought after for weekend parties.

Then, there is young Mister Aberdale and his sister whose family I believe was nobility in England and who attends a very fashionable college not far from here. Their parents are abroad and Madam keeps an eye on them from time to time. Two cousins of the Cabot's and their wives are here as well.

"Thank you, Anna. I think I am ready to go down now."

"I will tidy up while you are gone, Miss. Then I will help you to change for the afternoon activities."

Lily headed for the large circular staircase with its newels of highly polished gold each capped by a sculpture depicting the prey of an African safari hunt. Lily held the bannister as she descended, careful to lift her skirt ever so slightly and look about at the décor. Its opulence was noticeable, especially in the crystal chandelier that hung in the main hall and the many Chinese vases that sat on pedestals set on various exotic oriental carpets.

Elias greeted her and led her to the breakfast room, a smaller area than the formal dining room but no less decorated with cabinets of china and crystal lining the walls.

"Good morning, Lily. Come in and meet our other guests. Did you sleep well?

"Yes, Grandmother. Thank you."

"I'd like you to meet John Aberdale and his sister Agatha. Their parents are very dear friends of mine. And, next we have two cousins of the very distinguished Cabot family, Senator Henry Eldridge and his wife Elvira and shipping magnate Samuel Turnbridge and his wife Annabelle. Hiding behind his mother Mrs. Edward Winthrop is young master Edmond."

"I'm pleased to know you all."

"Please sit down and join us, Lily. We are just having a light breakfast before the hunt."

"Thank you, Grandmother."

Lily tried to listen and join delicately in the conversation as Miss Stanton had counseled but the talk was mostly about Boston politics and the next university to be built on Boston soil.

Senator Eldridge turned to Mr. Turnbridge. "How is the tariff war going down at the docks?"

"Henry, you should come down and see it firsthand. The longshoremen are threatening to leave the cargo aboard the ships and not unload. The harbor is so congested the merchant ships are threatening to dock somewhere else."

"I'm not sure what the Massachusetts senate can do but I'm going to the statehouse in two days for a meeting on the state of public education and I can throw in a hint or two to see if the mayor could use some muscle. We don't want another Boston tea party,"

"I'd appreciate anything you can do. Tempers are flaring among the longshoremen and the crews of the merchant ships.

"But, we must turn to lighter subjects. We have ladies present."

"Of course. And, I'm sure we can now hear plenty on the subject of gossip."

Annabelle Turnbridge was only too happy to begin. "Did you know that Jordan Marsh was able to get in the latest in Paris fashions? They keep them hidden in the back room for only those favored few to observe. They are hoping to get an invitation only fashion show in the spring.

"If anyone wants one Jordan Jr. has given me cards to give to a select few."

"That's very generous of you, Annabelle. I could use some new fashions to add to my winter collection."

"Of course, Elvira."

"Has anyone heard from the Tuttles? They have been abroad for six months now."

"They have spent much time in France and Italy sightseeing and visiting museums. But, Jasper Tuttle has business in Europe as well. It may be some time before they return."

Grandmother addressed Mrs. Winthrop directly. "Have you been in correspondence with them Henrietta?"

"Yes, Abigail Tuttle sent me the most beautiful postcard from France with a picture of the Eiffel tower. She claims to have increased her wardrobe immensely and is anxious to return so she can show it off. But, Jasper must take all the time he needs."

Senator Eldridge spoke up. "Excuse me, ladies, just for a moment but I must check on our young scholar here. How have your studies been going, John? Have you kept to the books even though your parents are away touring Europe?"

"I have, Senator. I have changed my course of study to reflect philosophy and history and especially art as well as commerce. That way I can be more useful to Father when I enter the business. Today's European merchants prefer someone who knows their history and their culture as well as understands the perils of sea trade so as not to be seen as a young country of brash upstarts as some influential European merchants continue to think us."

"Well, if you need anything, just let me know. I have plenty of connections at Harvard."

"Thank you, Senator."

Mrs. Winthrop turned to Lily. "Now, suppose our newest acquaintance tells us about her travel here and what it's like to live in such a rough land. It must be wondrous to finally experience some comforts and culture."

"I have enjoyed observing all the wonders of a city as advanced as Boston and have gotten much out of Miss Stanton's school for the short time my cousin and companion Carmelita and I have been here. Our travel by train gave us a chance to see much of the country coming east.

"But, someday Oklahoma will have the culture you have here. And, its vast amount of mineral deposits will be sought after.

"My Papa has provided us with a good amount of luxury. And, now that the railroads will be laying track not far from his mineral mines he will be able to provide even more and be able to ship his ore to Europe from the Boston harbor just as your merchants do now."

"But the territories are full of Indians. It must be terrible and frightening to live among such savages."

"They have their own ways. And, they don't like ours. They prefer to hunt buffalo than settle down and get supplies at the general store.

"But they live a life as they choose. Their tribes have ceremonies and rites like we do. And, they are good traders."

Grandmother spoke up. "I think it's time to prepare for the morning hunt. You gentlemen change and the grooms are waiting at the stable to set you on a good mount. The ladies can follow me into the parlor for a game of whist and a tour of the gardens and orchards. The perennials are in full bloom this time of year and the orchards are ready to bear a bountiful harvest."

Agatha Aberdale was kind enough to take Lily as a partner in the game of whist and teach her the rules of play. Although their score suffered, Agatha was very understanding and even invited Lily for tea when she could get permission from Miss Stanton to visit.

John Aberdale was kind as well. Croquet was the afternoon amusement and John made sure she had lessons on how to swing the mallet before she attempted to send the ball through the narrow metal wicket.

Grandmother was busy all through the weekend planning activities and making sure all was well with the guests who were having a marvelous time forgetting their cares of a very demanding week.

As Sunday evening approached Lily bade goodbye to Grandmother hoping she had made a proper impression so Mama would be pleased. Grandmother was seated in a high-backed chair in the library, a matching footstool at her feet. She was intent upon reading the "Boston Daily Globe" which she held before her. She looked up as Lily entered. "This is the only way I will get the truth about all my friends and my enemies too. You can't trust idle chatter.

"Lily, I'm glad you came. I hope you enjoyed yourself. I know this was somewhat a trial by fire but you came through it just fine. I hope we will visit as often as your studies permit."

"Thank you, Grandmother. I very much enjoyed myself and I look forward to returning."

"Anna has packed your satchel and Elias will see you to the carriage. Please do give my greetings to Miss Stanton and my best to your Mama and Papa in your next letter.

Anna has also packed some fruit from our orchards for you to take back and share with the girls at school. I hope you will continue to take advantage of your studies as well as you have."

"I will, Grandmother. Miss Stanton has promised to begin piano studies soon so I will have another accomplishment to add."

"Well, I will look forward to hearing what you have learned. We have a wonderful spinet in the parlor."

As Lily sat in the carriage for the return trip back to Miss Stanton's Boston was all lit up and the streets quiet as they passed through. The sound of the horses' hooves against the cobblestone echoed eerily through the silence.

Her sparse room was a contrast to the luxury she had lived during the weekend. She decided to unpack her bundles in the morning and hurry through her one hundred strokes of brushing her beautiful long earthy light brown hair. She fell into bed exhausted. She could hardly wait to tell Lita about her visit in the morning.

Chapter Fourteen

L ily woke early on Halloween day. Prissy Taylor had invited both Lily and Lita to her home for the weekend and she must ready herself before the carriage arrived at ten.

She packed and dressed her hair in a simple bun with wisps along the sides held by a beautiful shell comb studded with pink and white pearls that reminded her of the exotic South sea islands she had read about and chose a plain white blouse and blue linen skirt to complete her outfit. Lita arrived in the gingham her Ma had made before they had left with a cloth satchel she had stitched herself.

They were swept through the streets of Boston in the most elegant carriage and arrived at the gates of the Taylor estate in good time. Lita gasped as they passed through the entrance into what was one of the most lavish estates that lay at the edge of the city.

Prissy's father was heir to a banking fortune and chose to keep the family home on land that had been passed on for generations rather than move to Beacon Hill where the wealthy had fled to avoid the flood of

Irish immigrants escaping a potato famine and the Italians who came later.

"Oh Lily and Lita I am so glad to see you. Welcome to my home. I can't wait for you to meet my family." Prissy had broken all form of dignity and had come flying down the steps in front of the great stone entrance to embrace them.

"My brother Harper is here from school and can't wait to greet you. And, this is my dog Pepper. He has been my companion ever since he was brought here as a puppy." Pepper dutifully wagged his tail at the mention of his name but then bounded off to chase a rabbit that had somehow strayed from the woods that ran for many acres beyond the mansion.

Harper, tall and handsome, with blond locks perfectly trimmed in the style of the day and clear blue eyes that seemed never to cease twinkling was in the great hall awaiting their arrival and as they crossed its threshold it was plain to see that although his manners were impeccable and he was polite to all he was most taken with Lita. Lita, the image of Grandmama in her youth with her flashing dark eyes and ready laughter who had left a tribe forced to wander as outcasts to cross an ocean to settle in a strange new land for her part was struck speechless.

Prissy tried to fill the awkward silence with endless chatter and an invitation to meet her mother who was awaiting their arrival in the music room. "Come meet Mother. She is practicing on the grand piano as she does daily. Mother could have been a concert pianist but it was not deemed proper for a person in her social position to embark on a career so she entertains at the parties of her closest friends to amuse them."

It was plain to see that Prissy's mother did not hold to convention. She rose as they entered the music room and welcomed them with a hug. "Please go make yourselves comfortable. I will ring for Maddie and she will see you to your rooms.

"I'm so glad you consented to come. I'm always so happy to see Prissy's school friends. I hope you will enjoy the weekend."

Lily recovered herself. "I'm sure we will, Mrs. Taylor. Thank you for your kind hospitality."

Halloween decorations were everywhere and the Irish servants who had celebrated the holiday in their homeland where it had been handed down from the Celts carved pumpkins and made witches and ghosts with gusto. Prissy had promised bobbing for apples at her party scheduled for the next day and a pumpkin carving contest.

Dinner was a formal affair and Lily dressed in a beautiful green silk and lent Lita her light blue silk poplin with lace and a newly fashionable bustle in the back.

Prissy's father was present at the head of the table and her mother opposite. "Welcome to you both Lily and Carmelita. Prissy tells me you have come all the way from the territories. What prompted your journey?"

"Now, Bertie, perhaps we should wait until they have enjoyed their dinner before they get pressed with so many questions."

Lily spoke up. "Thank you for your consideration Mrs. Taylor but I don't mind informing those around me about life in the territories. I know information travels so slowly and the east and the west often have a limited knowledge of each other.

"We have traveled here to attend Miss Stanton's school. Education is much more primitive in the west as is living. My Papa grew up here in Boston and it was Mama's desire that I learn the manners and ways of eastern girls since I have the opportunity. Papa has done well as a prospector and investor and Grandmother comes from a very old family here. My cousin Carmelita kindly consented to accompany me as my companion."

"I've been on safari and have bagged many a jungle animal but I'm told the west is just as primitive as the African grasslands."

"In some respects the Indians might appear to be if you don't get to know them. But, they have tribal governments and celebrate rituals and holidays like we do and they practice a religion that goes back many generations.

"Their chiefs are born to be wise and they have many who counsel around them. They are wise traders but some are warlike and others are not. They disagree on how to approach the federal government and they are unhappy with their hunting grounds being taken away from them.

"The land is rugged and difficult for farming. But, the mines yield more ore than anywhere else and the forests, though rugged, supply the farmers with wood for their homesteads and beds and tables and chairs to furnish them with.

"Without large cities the mountains are visible and the prairies grow the most beautiful wildflowers and all different kinds of birds flock to the forests."

"It sounds like an interesting place. I'm glad you have come east so you can get to know us. Perhaps someday I will journey west. I have read an account of your Cross Timbers and I would enjoy the challenge to explore.

"Now, Harper, perhaps you can tell us how your studies are going. Have you put to good use your year in Europe?

"I did, Father. I talked to bankers in France, Austria and Naples. I became very interested in the Rothschilds who had an arm of their bank in many countries including France, Austria, Italy and Germany and many more. Their investments were varied and ranged from diamond mines and copper mines to railways and vineyards, all of them highly profitable.

"What set them apart was their firm belief that their banks stay privately owned. I think if we follow that philosophy and not give in to the investors who keep wanting to make us go public we will do well.

"I was listening intently to Lily's story of the west. I think if we follow the Rothschilds' example and invest in the railways and mines in our own country we can better the economy of this country and increase our own profits as well."

"Well done, Harper. And, now we must adjourn and perhaps take this conversation to the library while the ladies discuss more important things like fashion and the latest European imports in the parlor and perhaps later we can all gather in the music room so that our guests can enjoy a short concert by your mother."

Lily retired early to a guest room full of plush colorful furnishings and beautiful paintings while Lita stayed on in the parlor invited by Harper to view the coins, stamps and early-century swords he had collected in his year of study and touring Europe.

Sunday's Halloween party was a flurry of activity as girls arrived by all manner of beautiful carriages, some with costumes and all with masks. Prissy provided the masks for Lily and Lita and they all bobbed for apples and watched while the servants carved pumpkins at their direction.

As Lily and Lita were whisked back again to Miss Stanton's Lita couldn't remember when she had so wonderful a time while Lily basked in the warmth of their new friends and promised herself to remember to write Papa about Harper's observations on banking. Boston was lit up as they drove through the city and the gold dome of the Massachusetts statehouse not far from Grandmother's estate on Beacon Hill was visible in the distance.

Though Lily admired the skyline of the well populated city the vision of purple mountains, green hills, beautiful wildflowers swaying about in a gentle spring breeze and evenings under the stars nestled in a clear, dark sky began to creep back into her memory.

Chapter Fifteen

L ily was headed for the Aberdale estate for afternoon tea. Agatha Aberdale had made good on her promise and Lily was set as her guest. Her brother John was taking time from his studies at Harvard to join them.

She looked forward to the afternoon and getting acquainted with both Agatha and John. She had been grateful for their earlier kindnesses and envied their independent natures.

As the coachman drove full pace through cobbled streets the well-dressed crowds scurried about the walkways intent only on reaching their destination, oblivious of the sun that warmed them and lit their way, or the trees with their showy reds and oranges lining the city square or the squirrels scampering about underfoot anxious to bury their hard-won oaken loot for the winter.

The Aberdale estate was as palatial as Grandmother's but not as high up on the hill. The orchards surrounding it bore the most succulent fruit and the gardens were stunning with exotic blossoms vying with more indigenous blooms.

Agatha was waiting to greet her and brought her from the carriage to the parlor where tea had been set up in a beautiful and elegant tea service. "We must get better acquainted. I want to know about Oklahoma but most of all I would so much like to know more about you. Somehow I feel we are kindred spirits and will have so much to talk about. And, please call me Aggie."

John Aberdale arrived just as they were finishing tea. "Good afternoon, ladies. It's so good to see you, Lily. I'm glad you could join us even for so short a time. Perhaps you would like to take a stroll in the gardens?"

"Thank you, John. They must be so lovely this time of year."

Aggie spoke. "Mother prides herself in her gardens. She took first prize at the Massachusetts Horticultural Society's annual competition and helped found the Public Gardens. She would be delighted to have you view them."

As John led Lily out into the crisp autumn air she stepped into what seemed like a fairyland of flowers set about in a variety of exotic blooms. The rose garden was full of cupids in impish poses and fauns, the silly half-goat creatures that lent a magical presence to the woodlands of Roman mythology. Their depictions delighted Lily who was certain the little creatures with their impish ways could bring joy to any forest.

The Asian gardens with their red lanterns that glow in the dark and the narrow streamlet that ran through them lent a mystique to the carefully tended flowerless foliage. The European gardens with their lively French blooms and the ornate Italian, brought hues of all kinds and the colonial gardens a sense of history with little placards announcing the dates and settlements in which they were bred.

"They are beautiful, John."

"Well, it takes a special person to appreciate them."

As they strolled they came upon an arbor of dwarf chestnuts shading an intricately scrolled stone bench. "Perhaps we can rest a while. The asters are in full bloom and they surround us."

John seemed anxious to talk. "Lily, why did you come here? You are different than the other girls I've met. They are all so coquettish and silly and only out to lure a husband so they can oversee a social life and an estate."

"Mama sent me here to learn the ways of becoming a fine lady and perhaps travel to Europe to mingle with the nobility. But, I find no interest in that. There is so much of the world I haven't seen yet.

"Life in the territories is very much a daily struggle. Farmers work hard to pull crops from a nearly barren soil, Indians fight Indians and the federal government, and Civil War veterans hold a grudge against each other. Here there is a life of ease."

"You mustn't be fooled by appearance. Although we live a life of luxury and outward civility friends are wary of friends and neighbors of neighbors. The battles are fought through governing bodies instead.

"But, I would like to show you the cultural side of Boston. The art galleries and the symphony. Would you accompany me sometime?"

"I would be delighted."

"I too have wondered about my own path. It has been set out for me since I was a mere boy. Father was certain I must follow him into the shipping business but I have longed to paint. Whenever I see an interesting face or a flower that stands out from the rest I long to put it on canvas.

"I have dabbled for a time in a studio I set up in the stable annex. I have sworn the stable hands to secrecy. I have shown my art to no one but somehow I trust you, Lily. Would you like to see my amateur efforts?"

"I would love to, John."

As they strolled back to the annex, the garden paths filled with crushed stone, Lily admired the statuary. Graceful maidens with pitchers and sandals, Roman gods and Greek Olympians with robes. She wondered what they would say if they suddenly came to life and how they would view the world they came to be in.

"We are here," John announced as he swung open a rather large wooden door that led to a room unfurnished except for a rough oaken table, a few chairs and a large easel surrounded by tubes of paint, several brushes soaking in turpentine, and several blank canvases stacked neatly in the corner.

The odor of hay and feed drifted from the stables but the walls were covered with all manner of paintings from landscapes to still lifes and portraits of models in fine dress.

Lily gasped as she looked around. Never had she seen paintings so vivid and intense as if she could feel the taste of a banana in a still life on her own tongue or feel the wind of a stormy landscape or sense the elegance of a well-bred model. "Your paintings are beautiful, John."

"Do you really think so Lily? I wouldn't want your honest opinion to be clouded by your obvious good manners."

"I think they are as beautiful as what Mother has imported from Parisian galleries. But, hers seem to belong in a gallery rather than a home. Yours spring to life even on the walls of a rough wooden building."

"I must confess I am not altogether self-taught. I have studied in private with a painter who spent years in Europe studying with the masters.

"Someday I would like to go to Europe and study with the masters as he did. But, I know it is only a dream."

"Dreams have a way of haunting us until we listen and make them come true. Perhaps someday you will paint on the streets of Paris."

"Thank you, Lily. I will remember that as I toil over the books. But, for now we must return to the parlor.

Aggie will be thinking we have run off to another county."

Aggie was practicing the piano as they entered the mansion. Her soft and sweet melodious tones drifted through the open door of the parlor as they found their way back. She insisted Lily stay for a game of Charades, the latest rage borrowed from the drawing rooms of Europe. They all giggled over the antics of the others as they each tried to depict a simple object in pantomime.

She was returned to Miss Stanton's in style with bags and bags of fruit gathered from the Aberdale orchards and an invitation to visit again soon. She begged off studying for the morrow and fell into bed after the required one hundred strokes of brushing her long tresses with an ebony brush fitted with the stiffest boar's bristles.

She closed the drapes, the sky barely visible through the panes of the lone long window, hidden behind a skyline of very tall buildings. She fell into the bed, the soft down mattress already beckoning her into a deep sleep. As she pulled the comforter, its embroidered bouquets of violets a touch of elegance in the sparse and simple room, up over fine linen sheets she could see only visions of a sky with the brightest stars surrounding a new moon, shining at dusk over a purple haze that settled on the mountains, the prairies and the woodlands of a vast and untamed landscape.

She wondered what Wohali was doing now and what he was thinking. Was he gazing at the sky looking for a shooting star as they had so often done together or was he toiling over the sacred totems he carved to keep the beliefs of the ancients and his own heritage alive?

As she thought over the day she was grateful for her new friends and the comforts of Grandmother's home and Boston. But, as she glanced at the totem Wohali had carved she thought of his words as they parted. "You are a part of these hills as the trees that have clung to the earth that nourishes them."

She pulled up the comforter further, perhaps to shut out her thoughts. But, as she drifted off to sleep the forests and the prairies of the vast, untamed land of her birth seemed as real as if she were there.

Chapter Sixteen

A ggie Aberdale was chipper as she led Lily along the cobbled walkways toward Jordan Marsh. She was determined to be there before they opened at ten and be the first to view the new fashions just in from Paris at the start of the upcoming social season.

Aggie had a special invitation from Eben Jordan, Jr. and was anxious to see what he had set aside for her. The first in the country to open a department store Jordan, Sr. had connections to the best fashion houses in Paris.

As they reached the brick building that housed the most fashionable store in the nation the guards rushed to open up, leading them past darkened display cases crammed with the latest in ladies' scarves, men's cravats, and ladies' and men's hosiery ready to entice the first rush of even the most discerning early morning shoppers.

"Good morning, Miss Aberdale. Welcome to Jordan Marsh."

"Good morning, Charles. Is Mr. Jordan about?"

"He gave orders to make sure you wait for him in

his private quarters. He will be with you momentarily. He said you could have anything you want while you're waiting so please take the elevator to the third floor and let Emma know if you have any special requests."

"Thank you, Charles. Miss Paxton is my friend and will accompany me."

They were seated on a deep blue velvet divan, its scrolled cherrywood arms etched with tiny depictions of horsemen awaiting the hunt. A Louis XIV table of rich mahogany polished to a fine shine was set with Limoges china cups hand-painted with the tiniest tea roses, a beautiful coffee server that held the finest coffee beans imported from the best plantations in Columbia, and a silver platter filled with tiny fruit puff pastries.

"We must amuse ourselves. Eben has much work to do. Pleasing the socialites of Boston and keeping the sales force happy and well-groomed is a daily chore he does so well.

"He was adored as a child and grew up in the store following his father around but we must make no mistake. He is more shrewd than anyone when it comes to fashions and the taste of Boston society.

"He has all of Paris terrified and he has been known to back a designer he thinks will come up to his very demanding standards. But, his reputation for charm precedes him and all the society matrons still adore him."

As Aggie spoke, a tall, unassuming slender man dressed smartly in the latest fashions with perfectly barbered hair and a daunting mustache entered. "What brings you here today, Miss Agatha?"

"What have you got for me? Your invitation mentioned the latest fashions directly from Paris."

"So, you are anxious to outdo your competition and turn out as the belle of the ball. I think I have some very startling things for you. Marianne will model. She is a veteran of the Paris runways and a favorite of most all the fashion houses.

"We will have them altered to fit and deliver them promptly. When you are finished making your selections I would like you to be my guest for luncheon. Your guest is invited as well. And, who is she?

Aggie introduced Lily to Eben Jordan who made a courtly bow. "Now, Miss Lily, we must all seem incredibly strange to you. From what I read Oklahoma is mostly filled with Indian tribes who cannot get along with each other and prospectors protecting themselves daily from claim jumpers. It seems a wild territory far from the comforts of Boston."

"Perhaps. But, the beauty of the territory cannot be underrated. It is rich in the bounty of mines that produce the raw mineral that is turned into the gemstones you wear here. And, the coal that supplies your heat. When the railroad comes through you will get shipments directly to the Boston harbor."

"I must remember that. Perhaps I can find things that will interest your general stores. In the meantime, please send word to me if there is any problem.

"Aggie, I have included some plain cottons and linens since I'm aware of your work among the Irish and it wouldn't do to go traipsing about in silks and velvets. But, you should leave well-enough alone and keep to your duties among your own kind. The Irish are making inroads in the government and are about to drive us all out."

"They just want to improve their lot, Eben. The ward leaders are tough but they just want better conditions for the poor."

At that Eben disappeared called out by a very harried manager. As he left Marianne appeared in a ballgown of the most beautiful deep red velvet complete with bustle the latest addition to high fashion and chosen obviously to compliment Aggie's beautiful long dark raven tresses. The model's tortoise shell combs studded with rubies and diamonds completed the picture.

Aggie gasped at the beautiful ballgown and checked it off on her list. The fashions that followed were equally breath-taking and Aggie completed her wardrobe before noon. "Lily, please choose something. It will be my gift."

"I can't accept such an extravagant offering. You have been so very generous already. But, I get great pleasure just watching you fill your closet with the most beautiful fashions. You will be the star of the social season."

"You are very kind, Lily. But, you have done so much for us already. You have brought John out of his shell. He chatters about you incessantly when anyone will listen. I know he has been down about his studies. He would prefer to spend all his time at the symphony and the art galleries. But, his future was set for him a long time ago. And, it will bring him good fortune if he will only stay with it and take an interest."

"There are not many so fortunate as to be the heir to one of the biggest shipping companies in the world. But, I fear that John's reasons are different. I believe he studies to please your father who he does not want to disappoint. And, the conflict has brought him a great deal of gloom and confusion.

"But, he has been a wonderful companion to me and tries to show me the side of Boston that means so much to him. And, Aggie, you have shown me such kindness and generosity since we met at Grandmother's. I am grateful to you both."

"It was a good meeting for both of us. When you arrived we were certain Oklahoma was filled only with aborigines and outcasts and renegades from a more civilized society. You have broadened our slim knowledge of our western territories."

"John will find his way when he gathers more knowledge of the world. The best intentions for the future are often interrupted by fate. Papa was groomed to take over the most successful fabric factory in Boston but he left to strike out on his own. He never divulged the reason except to say he had suffered a grave personal disappointment but he has never regretted his decision."

"Well, we must go and wash up. Our luncheon should be served soon. There is a washroom just around the corner."

The lavatory in the Jordan Marsh personal quarters was as lavish as Lily had ever seen. It was cared for by a maid who handed them monogramed towels and floated fresh lilies in the bowls set next to the marble sinks for fragrance.

The luncheon was equally lavish. Hors d'oeuvres of pate de fois gras and caviar preceded a poached salmon set in aspic, tiny roasted potatoes and baby peas mixed with slices of the rare white truffle mushroom. Dessert was a perfectly baked chocolate soufflé set in a small pool of crème fraiche accompanied by a choice of freshly dipped truffles. Chilled white wines from the best regions of France were poured with every course.

Eben Jordan poked his head in. "Ladies, I have ordered a carriage for your safe return. I hope you enjoyed your luncheon. Aggie, we are expecting the latest fragrances in from Italy and France any day now so I will let you know when they arrive."

"Thank you, Eben. The luncheon was delicious.

"Lily, would you mind if we made a stop on the way? I would like to look in on a child I have been caring for."

"Of course not, Aggie, I would be glad to tag along."

Aggie gave directions to the coachman and settled back on the plush plum velvet seats as the carriage took a sharp turn out of the shopping district and onto narrow rutted dirt roads, by dilapidated houses, and children playing stick ball and kick the can as muddy waters rushed along toward a series of broken gutters.

As the carriage stopped, Aggie alighted, mindful of her petticoats and the hem of her silken frock. A woman with disheveled red hair and a ready smile answered the door. "Oh, it's you, Miss Aggie. What a nice surprise. Please come in. Would you like some tea?"

"I don't think we will have time today, Eileen. But, thank you for your kind offer. This is my friend Miss Lily Paxton."

"How do you do, Miss Lily? It is nice to meet you."

"I'm pleased to meet you as well."

"You are very welcome to our humble home but pay no mind to the chipping paint and the doors falling off the broken hinges. My Timothy works such long hours down at the docks he can barely sit to eat his supper before he falls asleep."

"How is Liam today, Eileen?"

"He is no better but he is no worse. I take that as a good sign. Mrs. O'Malley next door thinks it is the fever. She says her Colin was struck when he was just a lad and she covered him in cool cloths and fed him spoonfuls of broth. He got worse before he got better and she prayed a lot but now he's a healthy lad of fourteen.

"I've tried to keep the other bairn away from Liam. But, my Caitlin is looking a little pale."

"May I see Liam?"

"Of course, Miss Aggie. He asks for you every day. He looks forward to your visits."

Aggie opened the door to a tiny closet of a room that held a single bed. A young freckle-faced boy, his mop of red hair askew, lay listlessly under the cover of a once hefty woolen blanket, now worn thin from years of use. "Hello, Liam. How are you today?"

"Miss Aggie. You did come to see me. I knew you would be back."

"Have you played with the toy clown I gave you?"

"Yes, Miss Aggie. I can get him to do lots of tricks."

"Have you practiced the game of marbles I taught you?"

"Oh, yes. I can shoot real straight now. But, I can't play with my friend Patrick until I'm better."

"Well, I'm sure you'll be out on the street beating all the other boys before we can say Jack Robinson."

"Who's Jack Robinson?"

"I don't know, Liam. But, maybe we can make up a story about him next time I visit."

"I don't want to beat Patrick, Miss Aggie. He's my friend."

"That's very kind of you, Liam. Maybe you can show him the tricks you can make your clown do."

"I think he'd like that. Patrick will laugh. Patrick laughs a lot when we do funny things."

"I have to go now, Liam. But, I'll visit again soon. You get a lot of sleep and make sure you take your broth."

"I will, Miss Aggie. I think I'm tired now."

As they were whisked away in the luxury of the Jordan Marsh carriage, Aggie chatted about the upcoming social season and hoped Lily would be a part of it. As they gazed out of the carriage window a strong wind came up, blowing the last leaves of fall from the elms that lined the roadways leaving their branches as bare as a newly-planted tree. It was plain to see that winter was now upon Boston.

Chapter Seventeen

L ily could see the snowflakes through the long casement window of her room as Lita sat on the edge of the bed enraptured with Harper Taylor. Icicles hung from the eaves of the rooftop in fascinating patterns.

"Lily, I have never met anyone like Harper. He treats me with the greatest respect."

"Well, he is a gentleman. But, I know he has a reputation with all the best families for courting the ladies and never mentioning marriage."

"It is enough for me to just visit with him in the parlor. We laugh and talk and we are so gay with each other. The hours slip away too quickly before he must be off."

"It was plain to see he made no secret of his feelings for you the day we met. But, Harper has had his future set for him from his youth and it is not clear how a girl raised in the territories would fit that."

"We never talk about what might be. I just enjoy his company and he mine."

"You must give it time to see whether you are just another dalliance for Harper. I suppose keeping company in Miss Stanton's parlor is innocent enough but you must be watchful of his behavior at all times. Any changes will alert you to his intentions."

"I will be mindful, Lily. I am certain with your advice I will make a proper decision."

"We must hurry if we are to be ready when John and Harper arrive. We must dress warmly. The snow has been falling all day and I can see from our window the drifts are piled almost as high as we are."

"It was kind of John to invite Harper and me to dinner and the symphony. I have only heard the sounds of the symphony on Miss Stanton's phonograph when she prepares her lessons for harp and piano."

John arrived with Harper in tow as the parlor clock struck five. Harper looked dashing in a dark dinner jacket and top coat set off by a bright red satin vest while John looked proper in tweed. Both held their top hats in hand as they entered and announced their presence.

Both Lily and Lita had dressed in furs to keep them from the chilly night and had added hats with a variety of ribbons and feathers in honor of the occasion.

John offered his arm to Lily and Harper to Lita. John took the lead. "Shall we go, ladies? I hope the carriage I have brought will offer some comfort on such a snowy evening."

He helped Lily onto the plush red velvet seats while giving directions to the coachman. Harper and Lita came aboard and Lily heard the familiar clip clop against the cobblestone of the gaslit streets along with the rhythm of carriages passing at full speed on their way to an evening of exciting entertainment.

As the sun set and the moon rose the city looked more alive than ever, its lights a beacon against a darkened sky.

The Union Oyster House was the oldest restaurant in Boston and had served the likes of George Washington, Benjamin Franklin, and Paul Revere. Lily tried to imagine what they had looked like and what they had ordered when they had dined there.

John ordered for them all and the waiter, a serious proper gentleman with perfect manners, brought platters and platters of fresh cooked fish no doubt brought in that morning directly from the Boston harbor. Oysters, lobster, clams and mussels all vied for space on others. A hearty chowder to warm them preceded the entrees and wine and ales flowed to wash it all down.

John launched into the problems at the docks and Harper chimed in. "The fishermen refuse to bring in their catch with anything other than their small dory boats. Our ships' captains all complain that they are only in the way and are a nuisance when trying to dock.

"The fishermen pull rank and claim to have been here first but the shipping companies claim to bring in more money and business to the industries that drive Boston's economy and the fast growth it's seen in recent years."

"The banks earn more money from the companies that drive the shipping industries than they do from the fishermen but Bostonians are loathe to give up their fresh fish and their lobster. They would rather suffer an economic setback than give up their bounty from the sea."

"Tradition wins out every time. And, there is an air of romance in the fishing industry. Fishermen have been bringing in their haul in small boats for centuries."

"The banking business and I suppose the shipping business are in direct conflict with tradition and romance. So I imagine that argument will be going on for a long time.

"But, I'm afraid we must be boring the ladies. I have had recent news from Prissy that Miss Stanton has begun her lessons on piano and the harp. Prissy says that Lita is outstanding on the harp and has progressed way past the other students. When will we hear a recital?"

"Thank you for the compliment, Harper, but Miss Stanton says I am not quite ready. She says that when I am she will arrange a recital along with the other students and we will be allowed to invite guests."

Harper snapped out of his business talk and gazed at Lita with the greatest admiration. "I will be looking forward to that. I do expect an invitation."

"Of course. We are preparing a wonderful program. I think you will enjoy it."

"Lily spoke up. "It was so kind of you John to invite us to the symphony. It will add to the music training we are beginning to receive."

"I am delighted to do it, Lily. But, we must hurry. Scrambling for seats will test our manners even before the conductor taps the podium."

The streets were plowed despite the heavy snowfall and the carriage arrived at the Boston Music Hall before the bulk of the crowd burst in. As they settled in their seats a low hum filled the hall as friends greeted friends and others scrambled for a favored spot in the cavernous hall with its paneled walls reaching high to a latticed ceiling.

The strains of the music filled the hall with Beethoven, Mozart, and finally Chopin. Lily thought she had never heard such beautiful music. As she closed her eyes she could see herself on the back of a spirited mount across the territory prairies as the deep voiced instruments belted out a thunderous passage and she could hear the hum of the evening crickets when the strings turned to a soft and melodious one.

The audience gave a wild and standing ovation and John led them toward the exit and an outside line of waiting carriages. "We must test the desserts in my favorite tea room before we call an end to the evening."

The tea room was down by the wharf and an obvious favorite of the Harvard crowd judging from the carvings in the small, round wooden tables. The owner, a small Irish woman with red hair tied up in a knot on top of her head, seemed used to handling a tough, diverse crowd that ranged from college boys to longshoremen, sailors, and stragglers from the nearby local taverns.

"Come on in, Mr. John. Take a seat anywhere. The place will stay empty this time of night. The sailors are asleep and the stragglers have made their way home."

"What can you bring my friends, Siobhan, that will tempt them?"

"We have a few fruit scones left and some small cheese biscuits. But, we have some of the best chocolate shipped in from France that the sailors save for me in return for a pint of ale. I can heat it up with some milk and cream from the island dairies and warm you all up."

"Siobhan, you have saved us from the bitter cold of a typical Boston winter evening."

The night flew by as they chatted and midnight turned to the wee hours of the morning. They parted with a full moon overhead and icicles hanging from Miss Stanton's sturdy front door.

Moonbeams streamed through the window as Lily prepared for bed, bouncing about and playfully darting from bed to dresser to the pomade dish atop the sturdy cherrywood dressing table. She laughed as they eluded her gaze and began to unpin the combs and the clips of her carefully coiffed hair.

She must keep an eye on Lita lest she fall prey to a society she was far from prepared for but for now she must sleep. She must be alert for the morning's lessons since Miss Stanton was determined to put her charges through rigorous paces now that the holiday was fast approaching.

Chapter Eighteen

S pring had come to Boston and the trolleys had returned to clanging their way down the streets of the city without the slush and snow plows to stop them. The trees were leafed out and the walkers had a bounce in their step as they made their way down the elm-lined streets.

John had recently taken up art lessons at the Museum of Fine Arts and was anxious to attend the opening of his teacher's solo exhibit and introduce Lily. As he escorted her through the large front doors of the imposing Gothic Revival brick building, he picked up his step as he drew her into the exhibit hall.

"Why John, how nice to see you. Thank you so much for coming."

"I wouldn't miss it for anything, Professor."

"And, who is this lovely lady who has accompanied you?"

"Professor Benson, this is Miss Lily Paxton. She hails from Oklahoma but is here to attend school and visit with her grandmother who as you know is one of your greatest patrons."

"Why, of course, Mrs. Paxton has been a generous donor and has kindly supported our venture when we founded the Boston Art Club. We are very indebted to your grandmother and we welcome her very lovely granddaughter.

"But, I expected you would be perhaps dressed in coarser dress and look much more rough and tumble than your delicate posture would let on. We get very few visitors from the territories."

"And, I have gathered, very little news as well from the reception I have gotten so far. But, I hope someday the east will recognize the territories for the value they bring and that we will work together to share our wealth and our expertise."

"Well, if you are an example of an ambassador I'm sure that will come about. But first, you must share with me the wealth of knowledge you must have of the landscape and all its resources. I have longed to paint such a rugged territory and perhaps someday I will."

"The land is vast and open. There are no cities to clutter the landscape as there are in the east. The prairies stretch for miles and the scent of the wildflowers fills the air.

166

"The ground is rich in minerals and the forests are filled with wood and game. The mountains stretch toward a horizon that is endless.

"Perhaps you will visit one day and see for yourself. You would be a welcome guest."

"I would be honored and I might just take up such a kind invitation. But first, you must browse the paintings and indulge yourselves with tea and cookies which the patrons have so generously provided."

Frank Weston Benson's paintings were beautiful and filled with the discipline he acquired from the masters he studied with in his many years of travel in Europe. But, Lily could sense John's passion and the urgency he must feel to put on canvas what he had bottled up for so many years in a life he had never chosen.

As they searched for the refreshments a young man, rather pale and thin, but handsome in his attire with a pencil mustache and very stylishly barbered hair came upon them. "Bonjour, monsieur and mademoiselle. Can you direct me to the refreshment table?"

"Well, perhaps we can find it together. It seems to be eluding us too. My name is John Aberdale and this is Miss Lily Paxton."

"I am honored to meet you both. My name is Andre Boujere. Count Andre Boujere to be exact. I have just arrived from Paris but hastened here to lend support to Mr. Benson. We met quite by accident when he was a student at the Académie and I at the Sorbonne. We shared many good times together as students do.

"But, if you can keep a secret in my rush I have not dined and I was attempting to sneak off with a few of the patrons' cookies to tide me over until I come across a more proper dining experience."

"Perhaps we can leave the cookies intact and invite you for luncheon. I know a small tea room nearby that I think would do. Please join us as my guest."

"I'd be honored. Thank you for rescuing me from a very brash act."

The scent of spring was in the air as they strolled toward the tea room, the soft breezes gently whipping at Lily's skirts and slightly ruffling the curls along her forehead. Birds chirped noisily in the newly leafed-out trees that lined the walkways and stray pigeons waddled about in search of tidbits lost by a distracted stroller. Andre lost his top hat to a sudden gust of wind sending them all into gales of laughter as he narrowly rescued it from the wheels of a passing carriage.

"I will miss spring in Paris but it will be interesting to get to know Boston. Frank spoke so highly of it."

"He also was taken by Paris and its charms. He has many paintings from the years he spent there. His scenes of Paris make me yearn to set up an easel as he did. But, my present responsibilities keep me busy here."

"Perhaps one day you will visit. You will be very welcome as a guest at our chateau. My father has been patron to many artists and has a small gallery along the Left Bank. He has made the reputation of many a struggling artist if he believes in them."

"I hope someday I will be able to fulfill that ambition. Now I see we have reached our tea room. I must find Minerva and coax her into parting with the special menu she keeps locked up in her kitchen for her favored guests."

The table John chose was a lovely one set off to the side in the corner. The white lace tablecloths gave a delicate touch along with the lovely silver and place settings and the matching lace curtains fluttering along the open windows let in the fresh scent of spring air. One red rose sat in a small china vase lending hope to the season of perpetual rebirth.

"What'll it be, Mr. John? We're quite busy today but we still have time for one of our most favorite customers."

"Thank you, Minerva. What can you whip up for our guest who is visiting from France? It is hard to compete with a country that has hundreds of years of tradition behind it."

"I will set before him the cheeses of Greece which he can wash down with the pleasant flavor of ouzo fermented in the best provinces of the country. I have made friends with a Greek sailor who brings me gifts from his family farm when he gets leave.

"I will add to it the heartiness of an Irish stew I have had simmering for hours and a choice of French pastries to round it all out with a strong Brazilian coffee."

Andre spoke. "That sounds like a real treat. A taste of so many cuisines will add to the education of my palate.

"Now, we must attend to the needs of our lovely companion. Lily, you must give me a full picture of your background. You must be a favorite here during the social season."

"I am a visitor to Boston like yourself. I come from the Oklahoma territories."

"And, what is a territory?"

"It is land that has not been brought into the union of the United States. The settlers of a territory must vote to apply for acceptance and there are too many warring factions for anyone to agree."

"Well, it's most fortunate that you have chosen to visit Boston. Otherwise, I never would have met you. What is the purpose of your visit?"

"I am here to study at Miss Stanton's School for Girls."

"Well, you must come to France for a visit as well. There you will be able to test your education and even take it a step further as so many of our noble families still practice the art of courtliness."

"I will keep such a gracious invitation in mind."

"And, John, what keeps you here in Boston?"

"I am the heir to a large shipping fortune and must work to be valuable to my father who inherited it as well. Our family has noble lineage by way of England but here there are no privileges so we must live as others.

John pulled from his waistcoat pocket a small tintype. "I carry with me the likenesses of my family. My parents travel often and it helps me to keep the memory of my responsibilities."

"Your parents are striking. They must be formidable and this likeness a comfort. But, who is that beautiful creature along with them?"

"That is my sister Agatha. Right now I am her only protector since my parents are both abroad."

"I must meet her."

"She is not interested in gentlemen right now. She finds the social scene a bore and is more interested in charity work than possible courtship."

"But, it would be a waste to let such a beautiful creature about without the proper companionship."

"Her youth would put her out of the running as companion to a man your age. You have at least a decade on her if not more."

"But, perhaps age is a benefit if it comes with wisdom."

"I shall put it before her but you must not live with hope in the matter."

"I am grateful for at least that small concession. And, now, I must find a way to repay you for your kindness. I insist you be my guests at a dinner I will be hosting for Frank Benson.

"We have an English branch of the family that emigrated here a few generations ago. They have a large estate not far from here and I am told I am welcome at any time. I intend to take them up on it.

"It has been my pleasure to meet you Miss Lily and John I thank you for your generosity and your kindness to a stranger. I look forward to spending more of my visit getting to know you better."

As John returned her to Miss Stanton's they were both quiet musing on a chance meeting they never expected. Lily smiled slightly to herself as she thought about John's brotherly protection but thought also that Andre's persistence was certain to win over John's most valiant attempts at resistance.

Chapter Nineteen

L ily stood on the sands of Cape Cod surveying the ocean. Miss Stanton's School for Girls was on holiday for the summer and Grandmother had insisted Lily spend it with her.

Grandmother's summer estate was more than palatial inside with a grand ballroom, a grand balustrade, stained glass windows that reached from ceiling to floor and sixteen fireplaces to ward off the chill of the evening ocean breezes. The outside was clapboard to mirror the simple fishing village that surrounded it.

Grandmother was planning to show Lily off when the social season began and to this end had imported a proper wardrobe which went from the latest in bathing fashions to the most fashionable ballgowns from Paris. She had invited Lita as her companion as well.

The house was full of guests on the weekends, mostly the newly wealthy who summered here from their mansions in New York. John and Aggie were frequent guests and Harper and Prissy as well.

Lily shaded her face with her hand upon her forehead as she looked out to sea. The ocean liners in the distance were hazy but the sailboats much nearer lent a grace to the magnitude of the ocean as they took advantage of the cool ocean breezes.

Seagulls trotted about the shore looking for food and clucking to chase the smaller birds away from their morning meal. Lily longed to wade in the rougher ocean waters as they lapped along the beach but realized it was improper for a lady to lift her skirts.

The waters changed their hues as they rushed out to sea, headed for a misty horizon and perhaps eventually the shores of distant lands. Lily wondered what life must be like on the other side.

"A penny for your thoughts."

"Oh, John, I was certain everyone was still abed. I tiptoed about so as not to disturb the other guests.

"I was anxious to take the salt air especially in the cool breezes of early morning. The sunrise is most beautiful over the ocean."

The sun shone bright above them, gentle breezes playing with the few strands of hair that had managed to escape the clasp of Lily's simple hair-do, and the winds whipping about her skirts as she stood. "Lily, you must stand there. You are the perfect seaside model. I know someday I will paint you."

"I would be honored, John."

"But, now we must explore this forsaken island. The ghosts of departed generations seem to haunt us as we wake."

"The servants speak in hushed tones of tales they have heard handed down through the generations. But, there is no proof and not a single remnant to show there was life before the wealthy moved in."

"I think if we are patient something will turn up. But, in the meantime, we must find a resting spot. That woods up ahead will do nicely."

John led Lily to a fallen log and helped her up. The rays of the sun shone through the treetops as they sat. "Lily, I must ask for your advice. Andre pesters me with requests to court Aggie but I put him off with feeble excuses."

"Perhaps you can compromise, John. You might allow him access to your estate but keep him under a watchful eye with constant chaperone."

"I have thought of that. But, Aggie is as skittish as a young filly when it comes to the thought of courtship and Andre is persistent in wanting to know her."

"Then, perhaps you can invite him to dinner with a number of friends and acquaintances. Such an event will hold no promise of courtship and you will have fulfilled Andre's wishes for a meeting."

"I believe that sounds like the best solution. Mother has always been here to watch out for Aggie but I know Father's business has kept him travelling for longer than he would like."

"You have been a good brother to Aggie."

"Now that she is of marriageable age it has become more difficult. She is more interested in her charities than she is in finding a husband."

"I'm sure when the time is right she will give in. But, she has so much more living to do before she settles."

"I see that you are right. Her face just lights up and is all aglow when she speaks about the poor and the downtrodden. She is a natural advocate for the poor.

"The unions have tried to organize the dock workers. Father will find it difficult to keep them down when he returns.

"Aggie has gotten word of their organizing and thinks it a good idea to better the lives of the Irish. They have found work with the railroads as well but the big companies are so interested in being the first to get the big contracts that they work the Irish so hard that there's no safety for the men who lay track. They've lost a lot of Irishmen in the rush to move west."

"I see that's the plight of the family Aggie watches over. Women must do all the work at home if they can't find work themselves because the men work long hours for little pay."

"I forbid Aggie to attend union meetings or to get involved in any way. It would ruin her chances for a suitable marriage because gentlemen do not prize ladies who are that ambitious outside of being the mistress of a household."

"I understand that you are just trying to protect her. But, Aggie has a mind of her own and I know she will be using it. But, I also know she will be considerate of you and your concerns for her as well."

"Well, you have set my mind at ease as I know you have been a good friend to Aggie."

"And she to me. Aggie has been most generous as you have, John. I am very grateful."

"Well, we both have prized your company. It has been good for both of us to quell the wrong illusions we have had about the territories and learn that all who have settled the west are not barbaric or uncivilized."

As they spoke, a small, wizened man appeared from out of the thicket behind them, old beyond his years, a walking staff and a rather scruffy dog beside him. "Who are you?"

"I am John Aberdale. I am a guest of Mrs. Paxton who owns this estate. Who are you?"

"I am Eldon Rutherberry. I used to fish these waters but now I fix things for the Paxton estate. In return Mrs. Paxton lets me stay in my small cabin yonder."

"It's nice to meet you, Mr. Rutherberry. What stopped you from fishing?"

"I used to get up before dawn and haul in the fish like the best of 'em. But, when my knees gave out I was forced to give it up.

"My missus used to look out for me every day atop the widow's walk 'til I came home. But, she's gone now. Taken suddenly ten years by now by my count. I miss my Bessie every day. How that woman could cook. She could make cod melt in your mouth like it was butter."

"The Paxton estate looks in good order. You must do your job well.

"What can you tell us about the history of this place?"

"The Cape's seen a lot of people come and go. The Injuns left run off by the English and the English didn't know a lick about farmin' so they left the island to the fishermen and the whalers. It's peaceful here, especially when the summer folk leave.

"Well, I'll be on my way. There's a lot to do when the guests start pourin' in."

He left as quickly as he had appeared, a little gnome-like man who for all his bluster seemed to hold the mystery of this once-forsaken island in the palm of his hand.

"We must return back before Grandmother notices our absence. She is anxious that I meet her New York guests who have come into wealth with the railroads almost overnight.

"She believes the New York tycoons are rough around the edges and courser than the Boston elite. But, she thinks their mingling with the more cultured of Boston will rub off.

"It is said that when the New Yorkers struck it rich they surpassed the wealth of the more staid Bostonians. I believe Grandmother is searching for eligible young gentlemen to attend the ball she will give on my behalf when the summer social season begins. I believe she sees every matron on the island as a competitor and is anxious to establish herself as the matriarch of the Cape Cod social season."

As they strolled back to the summer house, each silent with their own thoughts, the sun at its highest, the waters glistening as they rushed up on the pristine sands baking in its warmth, salt water spray filled the air and doused them with its mist as gentle as the morning dew. Lily was certain they would be restored to robust health before their return to a life of rounds of dinner parties, late nights at the concert halls, and vying for space on the crowded walkways of a city nearly bursting at its seams with the influx of travelers from distant lands seeking asylum in a city they had heard was rich with hope.

Chapter Twenty

L ily sat sidesaddle on a very regal mount as she set out to explore the nearly seven hundred acres of Grandmother's summer estate. She had invited Aggie to accompany her since Grandmother had been almost a surrogate parent to Aggie and John while the elder Aberdales were away on their European jaunt to gain better connections with the more established and wealthiest merchants on the Continent.

She yearned for her riding breeches and the simple hairdo of the prairies but she had promised to abide by the rules of dress of the eastern gentry. As such her riding habit was a plain black silk with petticoats and a feathered derby to match. Gloves and black leather boots rounded out the outfit.

Aggie looked more comfortable as she rode along in a long black silk skirt topped with a red velvet riding jacket and plain top hat. She carried with her a picnic luncheon the kitchen servants had packed and a canteen of deeply steeped tea.

"We must find a glade of woods or perhaps a lovely meadow to lay our blanket on. I will search for the proper spot since you have been the perfect custodian of our picnic."

"Your grandmother has charged me with being the guide to our eastern riding ways. She fears a return to what she calls the rough and tumble ways of the territories before she can get you properly introduced to the many young gentlemen she hopes will respond to the invitations she will be sending out for the ball she plans to throw to launch the summer social season."

"I'm not sure I'm ready for such attention. But, I'm anxious to please Mama who would so much like to be accepted by Grandmother.

"Grandmother had plans for Papa to marry into a proper Boston family and carry on her own family name. But, when he left she lost the privilege to arrange such a meeting and has always felt he married beneath his station. I believe she is attempting to make up for that loss with me."

"But, Lily, you cannot make up for your Papa's choice."

"I owe so much to Mama and I so much want to please her and make her happy. But, Papa's wishes are different. He was grooming me to take over the mines but he gave into Mama like he always has."

"I think you are making your Mama happy by coming here and studying at Miss Stanton's. But, in the end, you must listen to yourself or you will forever regret it."

"Aggie, I am grateful for your independent spirit. But, you must have news to tell as well.

"I do have some. John of course arranged a dinner on your advice and did let on to me that Andre wanted to have a meeting. I was at first against it but John pleaded his case because he so much wanted to please the benefactor of his beloved art teacher that I gave in.

"I was prepared to be as offish as I could and in doing so I dressed in very plain dress and made every attempt to make sure I was not cordial but Andre was patient and took every slight with the utmost grace that I could hardly contain my amusement.

"It was then that his patience won out. I could see that he was not fooled by my very obvious act and found him much wiser than I thought.

"It was then that I gave in and he has been a frequent guest of John's and we have talked and walked in the gardens and gotten to know each other.

"Lily, he is not like any other man I have ever known. Although he is French I feel like I have known him forever.

"He does not even mention courtship or plague me with such pleas and so we have become the best of friends with no promises or obligations attached.

"Unlike other gentlemen he values my independence and understands it. He even knows about my interest in the rising labor unions and has not shared that with anyone."

"I found Andre to be courteous, charming, and generous with just as much of an independent spirit. The last a most important characteristic for a person as yourself who values that trait."

"Thank you for your understanding, Lily. I fear when Mother and Father return they will not be so understanding. There is a recent trend in Europe for nobles whose fortunes are waning to chase after American heiresses. A fair trade to some. The heiress is bequeathed a title by way of marriage and the noble gentleman comes into a vast fortune.

"But, I have no desire for such a trade or to trade on my family wealth to land a husband. Andre has never discussed marriage and I value that. But, I fear Mother will be suspicious of his motives."

"Perhaps there will be a way to work this out. I know Andre was smitten when he saw your likeness. And, it seems that his family fortune is well intact. His father is benefactor to many established artists."

"Well, we must sit and enjoy our picnic. The day is lovely and I know the servants prepared some of their best cheeses and a newly baked bread and some ham that I know they have brought in from the best market in Boston.

"And, of course, some freshly baked scones to accompany our tea. We mustn't disappoint them."

As they sat, the grassy glade surrounded by black and white oaks, the ocean visible in the distance, and the rays of the sun warming them as they ate, Lily could only think of the many picnics she had shared with Wohali, his shyness when they first met, and how important it was for him to share his customs with her.

Aggie broke the silence. "John has told me about a strange little man who lives on this estate. I understand he was once a fisherman."

186

"Yes, Eldon Rutherberry. We will pass his cabin if we go a little further."

"I have been met with an idea for the Irish to supplement the wages that they earn. They make so little and work such long hours. I have been thinking if they could perhaps learn to fish and also how to farm they could get together and find a plot of land outside of Boston and learn to fish the waters as well.

"That way they could perhaps work their way out of the slums and to a better life."

"I believe John has set up a studio with a tenant farmer just outside Boston. Perhaps they would give your Irish friends lessons in working the land in return for help with sowing and tending their own crops.

"Aggie, the Irish are lucky to have you. But, we must head back. Grandmother is expecting us to dress for dinner and entertain her guests from New York. She would like to make a good impression and is counting on us to be at our best."

As they rode back storm clouds began gathering in the sky turning the serenity of its azure blue into a threatening mass of darkened gray as heavy winds began rising from the ocean, swirling the waters and the sands about, sending large waves lapping roughly upon the shore. Bathers hastily gathered their belongings and scurried for shelter. Sailboats, tossed about, headed for land.

A rare summer nor'easter was hitting the coast of Cape Cod. Lily, used to the warnings of Oklahoma twisters, called a warning to Aggie as she hurried her mount. They must reach the safety of the mansion and huddle behind shuttered windows until the unforgiving winds and the heavy rains that accompany them calmed.

Chapter Twenty-One

G randmother sat at the head of the table as she held sway over a very interesting assortment of guests. She had decided to mix her New York acquaintances with a number of proper Bostonians. She had invited Prissy along with Harper but had withheld his invitation until she was persuaded that it would be an insult to the matron of the Taylor family who were her bankers from way back.

Harper's reputation as a heartbreaker had preceded him and Grandmother had invited a very important New York politician whose family included three daughters of marriageable age. But, Harper had only eyes for Lita who Lily had invited on a whim.

Lily was anxious to catch up with Lita who had stayed as personal assistant to Miss Stanton over the holiday which brought a small stipend and she was proud to relieve Mama of expenses over the summer.

The rest of the guests included a few New York families with young men of marriageable age and a Boston politician and his wife who Lily had never met.

Luncheon was held in a small, informal dining area and dinners were reserved for the elegant, larger quarters of a more formal setting with carved panels, crystal chandeliers, perfectly polished wooden floors covered by an exquisite oriental carpet purchased during one of Grandmother's many travels abroad, and oriental vases set on pedestals surrounded by gilded objects everywhere.

Lily surveyed the luncheon room as the guests were invited to partake exactly at the time allotted by Grandmother. The décor was lovely despite its informality and beautiful paintings by Grandmother's protégés from the Boston Art Club hung everywhere. Lily was certain John's paintings would also find their way to the walls of the wealthy if he chose to follow his dream.

"We are here enjoying the ocean but I understand my New York guests prefer the rougher terrain of what they call the Adirondack Mountains."

"Yes, this is true, Mrs. Paxton. It is a rough terrain but we have managed to carve out of it some very large estates that take advantage of the clean mountain air just as you enjoy the restorative waters and salt air that the ocean brings.

"There we are far away from the congestion of the city and it restores our constitution as we hike the trails carved out long before we settled there and it brings back our thoughts with the clarity we were certain we had lost. Many an important deal has been forged in the thick of a forest or in a canoe paddling about in a very small lake or on a mountain top where you can see forever.

"We have many guest cabins and would be happy to host anyone who would like to give it a try."

"That is very kind of you, Abner. Perhaps some of my more hearty friends will take you up on it.

"We have not yet heard from our politicians. We have two states represented here. Is there anything our business friends should know about?"

"There are no important bills up since it is summer and many politicians take that opportunity to travel. But, as we both know coming from two different states our needs are different but working with the federal government is the same.

"It is difficult to persuade them to understand our needs when they see no difference in states or our land values or the influx of immigrants and migrants who fill our cities but bring so many differences.

"Many have not even traveled to see the problems we face but work only from their desks in Washington. Our representatives do the best they can but often the federal government overrides their best interests and they must let their constituents down.

"But, we must refrain from such talk as we have very lovely ladies present and we do not want them to be weighed down with such problems. Their gifts remain in running a household and at that they excel."

"Well, I will take you at your word, Edward, since I believe we must enjoy the salt air while we can. For the ladies, I invite you all to peruse the library where we have many of the latest novels from England and many from our own country as well.

"There is a colony not far from here where many of our more distinguished writers cluster and they are turning out some very interesting writings.

"As for taking the waters I have asked George to set up cabanas along the beach for all of you who request them. I would highly recommend taking these invigorating waters, cold as they might be, while we can.

"Now after you sample the delicacies of a Boston table please explore the grounds. There will be cigars in the library for the gentlemen and a piano recital for the ladies in the parlor."

Harper regaled the guests with witty anecdotes of his European travels and the New York mogul the wonders of railway travel and the many opportunities it was opening up as it pushed west. Lily traded witty remarks with the guest to her right and Lita gazed at Harper in rapt admiration as he spoke.

As the guests rose after the last of the Boston cream pie Lily signaled Lita and the two headed for a side entrance, giggling as they went congratulating themselves on their accomplished escape from Grandmother's ever-watchful eye. "Lita, we must find a place to sit and catch up. We must find a quiet spot as we did at home."

"Well, it was different there. I was trailed by the little ones. I miss the sound of their noisy voices as they clambered to be the first to beg a favor or get let out of a chore."

"Lita, you have done so well here. You must be the best harp player Miss Stanton has ever instructed."

"Thank you, Lily. But, I know Ma is plagued and overworked with my absence. She has sacrificed so much to give me this opportunity."

"I think you have repaid her. She must be very proud. Now, here is a spot where no one will find us."

As Lily laid a blanket she had wheedled from a laundry servant Lita spoke. "Lily, I must talk to you about Harper.

"I will burst if he doesn't propose marriage soon. But, I know why he procrastinates."

"Perhaps he fears his parents will not approve. Or, that he will disappoint his father and that his father might disinherit him or not allow him into the banking business."

"Harper fears nothing. He is the most courageous young man I have ever known. He says if his father disowns or disinherits him he will start a bank of his own. He has enough knowledge from the years he has spent apprenticing to his father and in his travels studying with the Rothschilds.

"It is that he fears a life of misery for me if I am not accepted. And, he says he cares for me too much to drag me into a life like that.

"Lily, I would rather face a life of misery than give Harper up."

"Lita, I am sure there is a way out of all of this. We must explore your choices. You are young. There must be many opportunities in your future."

"I could not live without Harper. He is the first young man to accept my background and not make fun of it.

"Lily, gypsies have been outcasts wherever they've gone. And, this country is no exception. But, despite centuries of ill treatment they have managed to keep their spirit and joy alive.

"You have seen it in the dances of Grandmama as she whirls about with her tambourine and her long beautiful hair flying about and her bangles jangling as she moves. You see it in the fiddles of our cousins and uncles.

"It is that very spirit that Harper likes about me. He says I have given him the one thing he has always lacked."

Lily looked at Lita, her usually flashing dark eyes as joyless as could be. "Lita, we will find a solution. I know Harper is working hard on one. He confides in Prissy and she tells me that despite his reputation as a heartbreaker that is in his past. He admits to being too cavalier with other young ladies but he never took them seriously. She is certain he would never hurt you."

As they returned to the mansion, strolling the paths of the few small woods as they went, the late afternoon sun filtering through the tops of the many young trees, Lily could only wish the best for Lita. She had struggled through the humiliation of being poor with the graces of a noblewoman. She knew value beyond wealth.

The sun began to set as they reached the house. Laughter and the sounds of gay chatter drifted through the open panes of the stained glass windows into the humid air of early evening as the guests took their sherry in the parlor and the kitchen servants clattered about preparing an elegant formal dinner. Lily was certain the conversation at table would prove to be as lively.

Chapter Twenty-Two

L ily stood on the deck of a very large deep sea fishing boat as it slipped out to sea. The breezes ruffled her hair and tugged at her linen skirt.

She had asked Harper to commission the boat for Aggie to bring aboard Timothy O'Leary whose Irish family she had befriended in the charge of Eldon Rutherberry who had agreed to give him lessons on how to reel in the best fish the Boston seacoast had to offer.

Eldon was in his glory when he finally got his sea legs and Harper was happy to be part of what he saw as an adventure. As for Timothy O'Leary he was anxious to try almost anything to improve the lot of his rapidly expanding family.

The sea captain tooted the horn at the small boats hugging the shore and Aggie grasped the rails as the waters got more choppy. Lily shaded her eyes as she looked out at the vast expanse and wondered what lay below.

Timothy O'Leary looked out to sea. "The last time I was on a moving ship was on the trip from our homeland. I sometimes wonder if I did the best for my family by leaving a land that was home to my ancestors for centuries before us.

"But, those who stayed faced starvation the worst anyone had seen. It was pitiful to see the look of hunger on tiny wee ones as their mournful eyes looked up.

"My Eileen was sad as she packed up the little bairn to leave the only home she had ever known but she plucked up her courage for the wee ones' sake and she keeps it up even though the paint peels from our humble home and I have no hours to fix it.

"Oh, what I would give to be able to get her a Claddagh brooch or a ring for the fingers she works so hard to scrub the floors and stir the Irish stew she scrapes together from the leftover scraps she wheedles from the local butcher."

Aggie spoke up. "Timothy, you have done what any good man would do. You took your family to a better place so they could thrive. Someday young Liam will grow into a strong young man and he will find his place like all those who have traveled to these shores.

"I know your Eileen adores you. I can see it in her face, though wan, that sparkles when she speaks of you or the little ones. Perhaps when the unions organize the docks you'll have a better life."

"I don't know, Miss Aggie. A lot of the men are scared to show up at meetings if the bosses find out we'll all be fired."

"It will take a lot of courage but if you all show up they can't fire you all."

"I don't know. There's lots more looking for work that can't get it."

"It's fear that is the enemy of the unions. But, if the men all stick together they can make change."

"I don't know. I hear from the men who lay track that those who have tried to go with the unions have been given harder work or punished in some other way or fired as an example.

"Almost all of them are family men who have so many mouths to feed. They are feared to lose their jobs and risk starvation for their little ones like what they left behind them in the motherland."

At that, Eldon called to the captain to put down anchor. They were at a good spot and according to him the sea was full of cod and mackerel and bluefish and bass.

"Timothy, you watch it now. Some of the good eaters you can pull right in and some'll give you a fight. The tunas will feed you for weeks but they swim like the dickens and can pull you in so fast you're under afore you know it. I've been pulled in by tunas and bluefish alike.

"Now, your rod is held down on the boat but it'll be in your hand on the docks and the bridges. Sometimes you can reel 'em in and sometimes you can't. It's best to let 'em go if they gotcha. We've lost many a fisherman because they were too stubborn to let 'em go.

"I've baited the line but you'll learn what bait to use to go after the fish you want. No use baitin' for a flounder in spring when they only come around in the winter. No use goin' after the black bass in winter when they come inshore in the spring. Leave it to the deep sea men to get them the rest of the year.

"I'm gonna cast the line and you watch real good. It's all in the wrist."

Eldon cast the line with an expert hand "You get it where you want it the first time around it'll be good eatin' for many a meal.

"My Bessie could cook up a storm when she had a good catch in her hands. You get your missus to learn how to cook up a catch you can feed your family for weeks."

"I think she'd welcome the change from begging scraps from the local butcher. She's real good at making something tasty that'll stretch when she has a mind to.

"But, it looks easy when you do it."

"You'll get the hang of it if you get down to the docks when they're biting. The small tunas are jumpers. The rest'll keep outta sight and give you no sign until you cast your lines.

"The cod'll keep you fed year round if you can catch 'em and the bass is great eatin' if you can reel 'em in. They sometimes come in at over sixty pound but they like the shore waters so anglin' from the docks and the bridges makes 'em an easy catch."

As he spoke Eldon got a tug on his line and he reeled in slow and easy with a huge striped bass on the end of his line flapping about as it hit the deck.

Eldon put his catch down below in the keep the captain provided for the tourists who hired him for the thrill of a tale they could tell the folks back home.

He handed the rod to Timothy who stood open-mouthed at the size of Eldon's catch. "Now, you try it. Take it nice and slow. If you get a bite don't let it rattle you. If they're pullin' you in hang onto the rail and I'll take over."

"I don't think I've ever seen a fish that size. Back home in Ireland our small village was inland from the sea. We heard tales of fishermen but we never traveled farther from our village than the local pub. Sometimes a stranger would wander in passing through and tell us the wonders he had seen by the seaside."

"Well, keep your wrist nice and loose before you cast. That's the secret of anglin' from the shore or even out in the deep waters when you don't cast a net."

As Eldon went on with his lesson and Timothy cast the line with a force Eldon hadn't shown him a huge albacore tuna went for the lure the captain had provided and Timothy went overboard faster than he could grab the rail. Eldon grabbed the line and the captain threw a life raft tied to the end of a rope, hauling him in in a flash.

The captain headed for shore with Timothy drying out at the end of the deck. Harper spoke to Aggie. "I overheard your talk about labor unions. The banks can't support the unions because the bosses the unions are trying to break are their customers.

"Banks never take risks and Father is very conservative. But, this country is moving forward in many new directions.

"The Rothschilds have taken risks whenever they funded a war not knowing which side would win but their patriotic nature got the better of them and proved them right.

"Your Irish friend looks eager enough and I know from our own Irish servants that they are anxious to get ahead in a country they are still trying to understand.

"But, they are making inroads in politics and are taking over their own future in some cases. I would be willing to float a small loan if they prove to be good fishermen and stick to it."

"That is kind of you, Harper. I know it will be a while before they can get the hang of it but it looks like Timothy O'Leary is persistent and has a will of steel. I know the other dock workers do too. They prize their families and are willing to work hard to get ahead."

"Well, it's been an interesting afternoon. The captain has kindly shown me how to steer this boat and has let me have a try at it so my lust for adventure even as tame as it has been this day has satisfied my adventurous nature which I have had to quell to satisfy Father.

"But, we must head back while it is still light. I promised the captain we would be at shore before dark."

Lily spoke up. "Harper, it was kind of you to agree to commission the boat. I think the lesson was helpful and I think Eldon Rutherberry has not had a day like this since he was forced to give up the life of a deep sea fisherman."

"It was a lesson for me too. I think we Bostonians give no thought to the fishermen who risk their lives everyday so our tables can be bursting with all manner of delicacies of the sea."

As they headed back, Lily looked at the sun sinking lower and lower in the skies as the moon rose over the swaths of color that signaled day giving way to night. Swatches of reds and purples and deep oranges were already beginning to show against the clear blue of the sky that seemed to meet the vast waters of a great and majestic ocean in the haze of a distant horizon. Lily let the soft sea winds ruffle her skirts and blow the strands of her hair about. There would be plenty of time to dress for dinner.

Chapter Twenty-Three

L ily pulled a favorite deep jade silk dress from her closet as she prepared to dress for afternoon tea. Grandmother had requested she take tea in the library and she knew her dress would be on display as well as her manners and her ability to hold her own in witty conversation.

She knew the deep jade silk was the latest in fashion and would complement the highlights in her earthy brown hair with its generous bustle, its tight sleeves finished in ruffled wristlets and its crewel embroidery of tiny roses and violets about the deep neckline and hem. Her diamond and ruby and emerald encrusted brooch added a touch of elegance and she took care to add extra perfumed pomade to her coif of ringlets along her forehead and long curls that hung at the nape of her neck.

She knocked at the door of the library and was let in by one of the servants. "Come in, Lily. You have arrived promptly at four as you were requested. Please sit down on the chair opposite.

"That was your late grandfather's favorite chair. We had many a chat after the servants had all retired for the night.

"His invention was making money as the first to industrialize textiles but the business end was keeping him up at night. He tossed his ideas about to me and though I could not help him he always told me I was his best listener.

"I could only ease his suffering by hosting parties for his business associates and making sure the servants brought him a piping hot cup of cocoa at the end of a long day. I also advised him on his dress since he cared less for fashion than the average worker who turned his looms having grown up with a simple country existence.

"But, my people came from a line of ancestors who went back to the nobility who arrived here from Europe a few centuries ago. Although he cared little for wealth and station he wanted to please me and bring back the status denied me by our marriage.

"I knew when he courted me he didn't have much in the way of family status. His family had lost much in the Revolutionary War. But, I knew he was as smart as a whip and had promise and ambition. And, by working together he proved me right."

"You must miss him very much, Grandmother. I wish I had known him."

"I wish you had too, Lily. I think he would have liked you. He admired spunk and I think you have a lot of that.

"You are your father's daughter. You have my Alfred's rebel nature. I can see it in your eyes. I hope you won't disappoint me."

"I will do my best and I am grateful to you for all you have done. I especially want to please Mama who sacrificed her very existence so I could have all the luxuries of a good education."

"I can see she lavished much on you. But, she comes from Gypsy blood and her people are not known for ambition. Rather for gathering around a campfire and making wild music while they dance about in colorful costume.

"My Alfred never had an eye to pick the proper young lady for courtship. He cared nothing for their backgrounds and fell in love with a girl from a home of poverty who worked at menial labor to help support her family.

"Her name was Betsy and she was a peasant girl and her family home was as modest as could be. Her father took odd jobs but was often remanded to debtor's prison for failure to pay his debts. He had a wanderlust they couldn't cure.

"She fell on hard times and was run over by the carriage of a very important man who cared little for the poor. She is buried in a pauper's grave.

"Alfred never forgave me for breaking them up. I took care of the father's debts with the promise he would never allow her to see him again. Alfred was certain that she was distraught the day she mindlessly ran in front of that carriage.

"He mourned over her grave and then suddenly left for the west and a life he knew nothing about. If it wasn't for your Mama sending news I would not have heard from him again.

"Now Lily, how do you take your tea?"

"With lemon and one lump of sugar, Grandmother, please."

"You must try the scones. They are fresh baked this morning. And the strawberry preserves are made from the strawberries grown right here on our own grounds. The servants pride themselves on picking the plumpest strawberries to harvest.

"Have you surveyed the orchards? They are our pride. Our fall brings in a harvest of the juiciest fruit. Many a guest has swooned over our apple tartlets and poached pear in aspic."

"I have, Grandmother. John and I discovered the most interesting woods with trails left from the Indians' time."

"Thank goodness my forebears ran them off before my time. The Indians are so warlike and know nothing about civilization."

"I think easterners do not understand the ways of the Indians. We have taken over their lands they have lived on for centuries.

"Pushing them farther west and taking them away from the only homes they ever knew confuses them and angers them. Some answer with war and some want only to get along with the new federal government and to make peace."

"Well, you mustn't be an Indian sympathizer. It is not popular among society and young men of marriageable age do not court young ladies who have such opinions. It ruins their standing with the very business associates they depend on to get ahead.

"It is best to leave opinions and politics to the gentlemen. Young men favor young ladies who are interested in becoming the mistress of a household and who wear the latest fashions with style and entertain guests of note with dinners they remember for years and especially throw the grandest balls of the season.

"Lily, I will be introducing you to the wealthiest and most highly-placed young gentlemen of Boston and New York. You must make the most of this opportunity for it will only come around once.

"I plan to be the first to send out invitations for a grand ball the likes of which Cape Cod matrons have never seen. I must insist you brush up on your dance etiquette for that is often how young gentlemen with an interest to come courting judge a young lady.

"If you need instruction on the dances of the day I will provide it. I intend to enlist the best dance orchestra Boston has to offer. Georg Henschel who has conducted the most world premieres at the Boston Symphony will be my guest and he has agreed to present his own composition as a world premier right here in our grand ballroom."

"I am very grateful you are taking such an interest in my welfare, Grandmother. Mama will be so pleased. I will try not to disappoint you."

"I will enjoy it, Lily. I excelled at the waltz and the quadrille at many a dance in my youth. Those were grand days. Your grandfather was quite a dancer himself. We were invited to the grandest balls of the season and we often danced the night away

"But, I have kept you long enough. You young people must enjoy the beach and walks along the ocean. The salt air is good for you and it will restore your health and return you to Boston ready to take on the burdens of completing your education."

Lily stood. "Thank you for tea, Grandmother. The scones were lovely and the strawberry jam most wonderful. I will be sure to observe the orchards in my walks about the grounds and check their progress as you suggest."

Lily left the library wondering how many young men would please her fancy or she theirs. It was a strange way to meet them under such formal circumstances but she was certain she must attempt to follow the rules of etiquette.

Miss Stanton had taught her charges the most popular dances of the day but she must pull her books of etiquette from her trunk and brush up on the many rules that preceded a trip to the dance floor. She sighed as she tried to repress her thoughts of days riding the Oklahoma prairies and the scent of the wildflowers wafting about on winds that tossed her hair and the sun that weathered her ruddy complexion.

The vision of Wohali among the gnarled post oaks of the Cross Timbers seemed as vivid as the day they parted. His parting words seemed to have been etched in her memory. "You are a part of these hills as the trees that have clung to the earth that nourishes them."

She had promised Mama she would do her best to become a fine lady and she would see it through. But, she was certain she needed to consult the totem Wohali had carved especially for her. She was in need of the courage the Cherokee beliefs swore it promised.

Chapter Twenty-Four

L ily sat on a bale of hay in the barn of a tenant farmer John had rented studio space from. John stood at his easel as he sketched her.

"Lily, you look perfect perched there. I will turn this into an oil my fellow students will be envious of."

"I'm honored, John. I just hope in time they will learn to appreciate you and your talent."

"Professor Benson has taken an interest. He has promised to help me if I can convince Father to lend his support for study in Europe."

"I'm glad, John. Some day you will be as famous as Professor Benson."

"I'm not sure about that. I admire him so. But, I do know that I would like to study with the masters as he did.

"Andre has offered his father as patron if I sail for Paris. But, it won't do to go against Father's wishes. He has set his every hope for the future of the shipping business on me."

"Perhaps his trip to Europe will soften him and his desires. It might be possible that this is just the right

214

time to have a company representative in Europe to expand the shipping business.

"This is still a young country. But, the Europeans have admired art for centuries and fill their courts and drawing rooms with the art of painters who find patrons in the nobility."

"Well, I will have my chance to put it before him soon. Mother and Father are scheduled to return home in a matter of months.

"I will be glad for their arrival. Aggie is pushing my sense of responsibility. She sees no young men but is only happy to be in the company of Andre."

"Perhaps they will work it out themselves. Andre is older but sometimes age comes with wisdom. He is intent upon letting Aggie do as she pleases."

"And, that pleases her. She has never enjoyed the company of a young man who pushes for a courtship or any formal engagement. She says she must live on her own terms before she thinks of settling down.

"But, she is getting older and with every passing year she loses her chances to all the coquettes who hide behind their fans and giggle incessantly."

"Andre adores her and her independence. I think they are both mature enough to work it out for themselves."

"Lily, you are a gift. You are one to always put my mind at ease."

"John, you have always thought of others before yourself. It was so kind of you to invite Lita and Harper along. You have given them a chance to talk away from the prying eyes of Boston society."

"Sometimes a brisk walk in the fresh air with the sounds of birds and the squirrels and rabbits scurrying about underfoot clears one's thoughts. I always envied Harper's dapper ways as he flitted about society with ease and made and broke courtships as if they were tennis dates and still managed to be the most sought-after bachelor in all of Boston society.

"But, he has been miserable of late. He can't concentrate on his studies and he has no interest in anything but your cousin Carmelita."

"Lita is miserable too. She is very concerned about Harper's future and does not want to hurt it in any way. She would get out of his life and go back home before she would do that."

"I don't think she has to worry about Harper. Because of his daring and casual ways people dismiss him and think him not serious. But, he is far from that.

"He is very shrewd in the banking business and his travels have made him a fearful competitor to the bankers in this young country of ours. The Rothschilds admired his spirit and his business sense and were happy to take him on as a temporary apprentice in their many branches that spanned the continent.

"But, he is most concerned about your cousin. He will not see her hurt and snubbed by the priggish matrons who can do nothing but gossip and judge without sizing up themselves."

"Well, perhaps they will be able to work it out so they will both be pleased. But, they haven't spoken to Harper's parents who may be very much opposed to such a match.

"Your friends the tenant farmers who have rented you this studio space have given them both a great deal of hospitality. I hope that will put them both at ease."

"Joshua and Phoebe have been very kind to me as well and have welcomed Harper as my friend. They have allowed me many hours of uninterrupted painting and have always made sure that I'm as comfortable as I can be.

"They have a hard life but they never complain. Joshua's father was killed in the Civil War and the family lost their farm. They are planning to buy the farm back in ten years or so when they have saved up enough money. But, that all depends on their crops and they depend on the weather."

As John spoke a small boy raced into the barn almost as fast as a twister readying to hit the Oklahoma landscape, his face, his cotton shirt and knee breeches smeared with dirt. "Mr. John, can I have a sweet?"

"If it is alright with your mother, Nathan."

"She says if I ask politely and remember my manners I can have one."

"Well then, I guess it will be fine. Why don't you take one from the box over there and take enough to give your brothers and sisters one also."

"Gosh, Mr. John. Thanks. I guess they will owe me a lot of favors. Maybe even do some of my chores."

"Why don't you think of it as being generous and maybe they will be generous to you sometime."

Jan Surasky

"Well, I guess so, Mr. John. But, I have so many chores to do."

"You are helping your mother and father get this farm that will go to you someday. And, you are helping to grow all the wonderful food you eat every day. I'm sure your family is very proud of you."

"Aw, I guess. I know Pa is proud of how I took to the harmonica. I can get everyone stomping their feet as good as he can."

"Where did all that dirt come from?"

"I was fishin' down at the pond when my new puppy Chester ran off with my bait. I chased him and caught my foot in a rabbit hole."

"Well, it looks like you had a bad morning. I hope that sweet will make up for it."

"It will, Mr. John. When will I see my picture?"

"When I am finished with it. It's coming along really well. You were a good model."

"Good day, Mr. John. I hope Nathan is not a disturbance to you."

"Nathan is never a disturbance, Phoebe. I didn't see you slip in. Nathan is a boy with lots of growing pains like every other young man his age."

219

"Yes, we have lots to be thankful for in the size of our brood. But, they are often a handful.

"I want so much for them to make good and to get the education I never got. But, some days, when the weather threatens our crops, it looks hopeless."

"They are a happy and healthy brood, Phoebe. I think with your help they will turn out just fine.

"I would like you to meet a friend of mine. Miss Lily Paxton I would like you to meet Phoebe Tarbell.

"How do you do, Phoebe. I have heard so much about your wonderful farm. I am so glad to meet you."

"And, I you Miss Lily. Mr. John has been so generous to the children. We are fortunate that he chose our farm for a studio to paint such beautiful paintings. We are honored indeed."

"From what he says you have been very kind to him as well. You have seen to his every comfort even though you have much work to do."

"I grew up on a dairy farm and there wasn't much time for frivolity. But, I used to draw every chance I could get, sometimes just in the soil with a stick and sometimes when I was more fortunate with paper and pencil my Ma used to slip to me every now and then. It is a joy to me to see Mr. John's paintings of our farm and the colors he chooses so carefully. I know it is a good example for my Nathan.

"But I came in here to invite you to supper when you are finished with your work. I would like your friends also to join us if they are willing."

"I'm sure they will be pleased to join us, Phoebe. It is generous of you to extend such a kind invitation to us all."

"It is no problem, Mr. John. We have been blessed with a good crop this year and some of our tomatoes and beans and peas have begun to ripen. We even had a good wild berry crop this year which I have been able to turn into all manner of pies and good old-fashioned New England muffins.

"I must go and prepare. But, if you need anything at all please let Nathan know."

The table was set outdoors with Phoebe's best dishes. Lily and Lita both tried to help but Phoebe insisted the children take their turns at serving. Nathan held court as the oldest but even the littlest at three was begging to help.

Harper entertained them with his European adventures and the children were all agog as he explained the games of their counterparts in the far reaches of Italy and France. After supper they all helped with the dishes and Lita entranced the Tarbells with dances and games she had played with the little ones she had minded at home.

A cool evening breeze replaced the hot and humid air of the day and the hum of the crickets wafted in as Joshua and Nathan played a harmonica duet. Dogs lay lazily around as they kept a watchful eye for scraps the smaller children slipped them when they escaped their parents' steady gaze. Joshua and Phoebe led a song fest of tunes passed down from their forebears and their guests joined in when they could.

The ride back to Grandmother's was pleasant as John opened the carriage windows to let in the fresh country air. But, the day had taken its toll. Drowsiness intercepted their attempts at lively chatter well before they reached the narrow roads that led to the clapboard mansion set atop a hill at the edge of a sleepy village a refuge for the lucky few from a city steeped in the swelter of summer heat.

Lily gazed at the still, dark sky filled with the brightest stars, some twinkling, some not. As she searched for one to wish on John was lifting her out of the carriage and Harper Lita. She knew she would hear nothing from Lita until morning.

Chapter Twenty-Five

T he grand ball room of Grandmother's summer estate looked grander than anything Lily had ever seen. The walls were hung with draperies pinned with fresh flowers at every pleat and golden ropes with tassels hung in swags along the entire ceiling. Crystal chandeliers imported from France lit the entire room and Louis IV chairs upholstered in various shades of velvet lined the walls waiting for weary matrons.

Lily was dressed in the grandest ballgown Grandmother could find sent from her favorite Paris fashion house and designed by the head designer whose name graced the attire of the wealthiest and most noble European families. Grandmother was certain it would bring gasps from even the most reticent of the Cape Cod summer elite.

Lily's hair had been dressed by Grandmother's personal dresser and she had been helped into her gown by Grandmother's personal lady's maid who had been with her for years. Lily wasn't certain whether she could move about with ease but she was certain her corset would stay laced because the woman was an expert in corsets and had insisted that Lily keep hanging onto the bedpost despite her pleas that she didn't think she would ever take another breath.

The orchestra was warming up set off to the side of the room and the musicians' attire was as elegant as the guests so as to more easily fade into the background but provide perfect accompaniment to the latest dances of the day. A light supper was set up in an adjoining room.

Lily looked about the room with a slight bit of trepidation. Grandmother had arranged this ball to introduce her to the most elite of Boston society. What if she disgraced Grandmother with a faux pas she hadn't covered in the many manuals she had studied on the etiquette of grand balls?

She decided to think of Mama and how proud she would be. Mama had worked Lily's whole life for a moment like this. She would put aside her worries and think only of the letter she would send describing the wonder of the evening and be sure to put in every detail as if Mama had been there.

Lily's gown swished as she circled the room trying to remember every detail its lovely light fabric of tarlatane imported from India made especially for stepping lively to the popular quadrilles of a fancy ball. Its puffed short lightly woven sleeves of gauze and its low bodice designed to set off the grace of her long neckline finished with the most delicate embroidery and its flounces pinned with flowerets everywhere set against the pale apple green of the fabric chosen to set off the lovely earth tones of her fashionably coifed hair held with a single rose.

"Well, Miss Lily, how does it feel to be the center of such an elegant coming-out ball?"

"Oh, Harper, you startled me. I thought you would be with Lita."

"I could not calm her nerves so I thought it better to leave that to the lady's maid your Grandmother so generously provided her. She has been talking about this for days because she so much wants to make a good impression for your sake, and I suppose mine, but she is certain she will trip or do something even more disastrous."

"I am fortunate to have a cousin so keen to be mindful of my welfare but I so much wanted her to forget her troubles and have a gay time. Lita loves to dance and she has worked so hard for the welfare of others."

"I will see to it that she doesn't have a moment's unrest. I will keep her as busy as I can until the evening is over. I know she has been practicing the latest quadrilles and Miss Stanton has been generous with her time in teaching her the very latest in dance steps."

"Harper, you are generous as well as being a young man with much compassion. I value your friendship and how kind you have been to my cousin. I hope you and Lita have an evening of gaiety and laughter you both so much deserve.

"Now, I must study the room so I will not disgrace Grandmother. I know she is counting on me to remember my manners and know the etiquette of balls as if I was born with the knowledge. I must mind my every move especially with the guests Grandmother finds the most important to her future welfare."

Grandmother appeared dressed in a ballgown befitting her matronly status. A deep blue set off her perfectly coifed hair and a beautiful diamond and ruby brooch handed down from her many wealthy ancestors set a commanding tone. "Lily, I hope you have mastered all the dances I set out for you. We will be meeting many important guests tonight and you will be very much on display. A successful ball is where many important matches are made and many introductions made that lead to future fortunes."

"I will be mindful of that, Grandmother."

"Now, we must receive over here. You will be standing next to me and we will receive every guest as they are announced at arrival."

"Yes, Grandmother."

The guests arrived with a grandeur Lily had not seen before, in carriages with family crests driven by coachmen with gilded liveries. Grandmother was every inch the grand and gracious hostess, greeting each guest with a pleasantry reserved just for them.

A light supper was served in the anteroom, heirloom china filled with the most sumptuous delicacies of the sea, heirloom stemmed crystal flowing with the best of imported wines and, of course, bubbling champagne for everyone.

Lily sat as she was approached by every available young man on the guest list, some so shy they were forced by their mothers to make an appearance. Only one hung back, perfectly attired, thick curly ebon locks well barbered but with a rakish arrogant grin that seemed to never cease.

"Miss Lily, may I have a place on your dance card?'

"And whom do I have the pleasure of addressing?"

"I am William George Lockwood III, but much prefer Willy."

"I am not at liberty to turn you down, Mr. Lockwood, because the rules of etiquette specifically state that I must not, but I must confess I think your demeanor rather rude."

"And, I must return, Miss Lily, that you state your opinion rather boldly, unlike other young ladies who hide behind their fans and giggle."

"Well, then, now that we have both made ourselves clear I have put you down for the fourth dance."

He bowed once more and turned and walked away, a spring in his step despite the rebuke she most certainly meant.

Harper danced every dance with Lita, who looked radiant and beautiful, her dark locks perfectly coifed above a lovely pastel gown of pale rose embroidered with tiny shells and violets, against all rules of etiquette. The fourth dance came too quickly and Willy Lockwood was at Lily's side promptly for the lively quadrille the conductor had composed especially for this occasion. He danced divinely, then bowed as he searched for his next partner.

Lily excused herself withdrawing to the sidelines, the matrons already exchanging gossip in very loud and exasperated tones. "I think it impertinent of Harper Taylor to break every rule of etiquette and dance every dance with that upstart from the territories. Why, she has no pedigree at all."

"I think you are right, Delilah. She is just another gold digger wanting to better her lot without breaking her back. Amanda Taylor must be beside herself with grief. She can't seem to hang onto that boy. Harper was promised to more young ladies than he could keep up with but he kept breaking every courtship. I knew Amanda was not good enough for Bertie when they married."

"Bertie is going to lose all his banking business if he doesn't take Harper in hand and pay off that upstart to disappear from Harper's life."

At that the orchestra turned to a lively new dance and drowned out even the loudest matron. Lily bit her tongue. She was anxious to rebuke the matrons but she knew it would ruin every plan of Grandmother's.

Just as she was about to make a decision Willy Lockwood appeared. "Miss Lily, may I get you some refreshments? Or perhaps a stroll on the veranda for some fresh air?"

"Thank you, Mr. Lockwood. A stroll would be welcome. But, I must not stay long. Grandmother was firm that I be in attendance the entire evening."

"Well, you looked like you needed to be rescued. Society matrons can be vicious."

"You are very astute, Mr. Lockwood. And, where did you get such knowledge?"

"New York society is newer and fresher than Boston, but it is decidedly as vicious in its attempts to get ahead at all cost. Matrons in their attempts to shore up their husband's business think nothing of others and very much only about themselves and their own interests. A young lady without the pedigree who has a mild and delicate countenance can be thrown to the sharks without their even noticing.

"But, I have a question and a request."

"And, what is your request? I would be glad to honor it in return for the favor of your rescue if I can."

"I insist you call me, Willy. I deplore the formalities and feigned pretenses of a society that is basically descended from apes."

"I can certainly honor your request. But, I must counter that there are many good people even in society. But, there are many bad ones as well where there is no hope of change."

"I bow to your much kindlier observations.

"The question I have is a more personal one. I would like to call on you if you would have me."

"I am honored by your proposal but would like your permission to think it over. Grandmother is very firm that all callers must be approved by her."

"Of course. I understand. She is only looking out for your welfare.

"And, now, we must get you back to the dance floor. I think it is in my best interest to honor your Grandmother's wishes."

The evening was over almost before it began, the gaiety left behind as the carriages departed. It was by all measures a success and the gossip overheard by the servants in the ladies' washroom was mostly congratulatory and often tinged with more than a little envy.

232

Grandmother retired without speaking to Lily but Lily knew there would be much to discuss on the morrow. She hastened to her room to find a lady's maid to relieve her of her corset.

As she peered out of her window toward the sea lit by the moon she wondered what Wohali might be doing about now. Had he forgotten her entirely? Or, like herself, did he peer at the moon and remember those beautiful moonlit nights when they sat under the stars and talked about their dreams for the future?

She must remember to find Lita in the morning. She would not repeat those grievous remarks she overheard, but she must be at the ready should her cousin need her to steady a vicious outcome.

She readied herself with the beautiful nightclothes Grandmother had provided. Lovely cottons and linens with all manner of embroidery and lace and flannels for the chilly nights as the sea brought in winds from the east. The scent of the night ocean drifted in through the open windows.

She stifled a yawn as she climbed up on the high feather bed away from the cares of the day. She would get prepared in the morning for the certain inquisition she would face at afternoon tea from Grandmother but for now she must sleep away the exhaustion from an evening of laughter and gaiety and keeping up with a set of the most inscrutable manners she had ever been faced with.

Chapter Twenty-Six

L ily stood on what was nearly the top of the mountain as Willy pushed on ahead, hearty and hale and excited to reach the top. She dug her walking stick farther into the heavy clay soil to gain her footing, its lion's head handle set with emerald eyes.

"Lily, come see the sights. The lake is so blue with the sun shining on it, the sailboats are the size of marshmallows, and the view is glorious."

"Just a few more steps and I will be where you are. I have lost Elizabeth and Margaret."

"Oh, they will be along when they have a mind to. They like to play games and hide.

"We must pick a spot for our picnic. James will be along with our lunch any minute. He huffs and puffs and does not enjoy hiking but Mother insists he accompany us because he is the strictest of the servants and she trusts him to keep us all in line.

"Maggie and Lizzie love to plays tricks on him but he takes it all in stride. I daresay he is fond of them nevertheless and I know they make sure he gets an extra present at Christmas.

"How is this spot here? We will dine on the highest mountain above what they now call Fourth Lake."

"It looks fine, Willy."

"I think we will not be disturbed here. Lizzie and Maggie will no doubt feed their lunch to the deer and leave scraps for the birds and maybe a few crumbs for the fox puppies they love to watch."

"They are delightful. I never knew what it was like to have brothers or sisters but I have cousins galore who love to pester me on holidays for a game of tag or roll the hoop. And they plead endlessly to be pushed on the tire swing."

"Maggie and Lizzie have a governess so they rarely bother me. But, before Father came into money we were pretty much left on our own."

At that James arrived, huffing and puffing but anxious to relieve his burdens. "Where would you like the blanket, Mr. William?"

Willy pointed to a spot very close to the edge but with a magnificent view. "Right here, James. That way we will give Miss Lily the best of the Adirondack mountains.

"Make yourself at home, Lily. We have all afternoon to explore."

As Lily settled on the blanket she looked around. The vista was beautiful and farmlands stretched below. But, where were the open prairies covered with wildflowers and the Cross Timber oaks so close together you could shut yourself out from the world?

But, here on the top of a mountain filled with evergreen trees you could feel the warmth it must give in the winter and the desire to conquer nature as well as the strength to hold your own in a competitive newly rising financial district in New York.

"Your father must find it an oasis of peace here."

"He does. But, he was always an outdoors man. He has been on many safaris and he insisted I accompany him on two of his longest trips to Kenya as well. But, I turned out to be a big disappointment to him. He was a good marksman and brought down his share of elephants and lions.

"But, when he tried to teach me I couldn't shoot. I couldn't see them as prey because they seemed so magnificent against the blue of the African sky."

"That must have been difficult for you."

"He tried to hide his disappointment but I could see it in his eyes. To him, shooting big game in Africa is a rite of passage to manhood."

"Well, you do have your role set for you. I'm sure he will be proud of you when you become part of his business interests."

"That's just it. I'm not sure what they are. He was a shrewd businessman from way back. But, it wasn't until he invested in oil in a part of the country that few had any interest in that his luck turned. Now, he searches for another lucky strike but for me that is difficult. I find it hard to foresee the future."

"Perhaps when you are working side by side you will gain more of an understanding of business principles. Before I left Papa insisted I learn the books of his mines and his railroad interests."

"I find no young lady who is raised in the east privy to that kind of knowledge. They are raised to be more delicate and feign lack of knowledge for anything but the fashions of the day, how to order servants about and how to raise heirs in their own image."

"The west is too rugged for that. Everyone is needed and Papa has always thought of me as his heir. But, Mama had other plans. That is why I am here to study at Miss Stanton's."

"Well, I'm glad you have graced us with your presence. You have made quite an impression on the young men who attended your Grandmother's ball. I seem to have a lot of competition."

"Many left their cards and there has been a steady stream of callers. But, I find none who are truly interested. Many are pushed for the need to please their elders and find a mistress for a household they haven't even begun to think of. Others flee when I tell them I must see the world before I ever settle down."

"Then I must rescue you twice."

"Well, I must confess your attentions have been welcome. They have gotten me away from Grandmother's watchful eye."

"My family's status and wealth could get me any young lady I desire. But, I too would like to explore and see the world before I take on any extra burdens like a family and an estate with the great responsibilities that come with it.

"If I confide in you my real intentions for myself would you promise not to laugh?"

"Of course. There is nothing laughable in what anyone wishes for themselves."

"I would like to go back to Africa and start a coffee plantation. And, protect the future of the magnificent wildlife that inhabits those grasslands."

"I find nothing laughable in that. It is a noble goal."

"I must convince Father first. There is nothing worse than a penniless young man from an upstart country thinking he can tame Africa."

"Perhaps he will come around. He seems to be interested in many different ventures."

"Meanwhile, I feed my love of nature here in the Adirondacks. The woods are a haven of peace and the animals ask nothing of you."

"It was kind of you to bring me here. I am grateful to your family for their endless hospitality."

"I'm sure Lizzie and Maggie have enjoyed your company. They often find me a trial and tease me mercilessly."

"They are just young ladies with the usual confusion of trying to find their place in a society they don't understand yet. But, I'm sure your mother finds them delightful. They seem to have a spirit that transcends the usual contrition young girls are often raised with."

"Yes, Mother has always let them roam free. But, since Father came into wealth she felt it her duty to educate them in the fine manners of the wealthy. Their governess considers them a handful.

"But, we must enjoy our luncheon before it gets nibbled on by the squirrels and the rabbits. The breads are wonderful baked by the local farmers, the thick slabs of ham and the cheeses of the dairymen a real treat."

As they ate, they were certain they heard squirrels about but before Lily could turn away there were two small hands about her eyes and a voice that said, "Guess who?"

"I think it is the bogie man ready to tickle you."

"I give up. You are too smart for us, Miss Lily."

As they packed up and got the young ones on the right track behind them Lily followed Willy down the long trail back to the rambling, large estate of the Lockwoods, its log cabin exteriors a contrast to the rough but comfortable interiors meant to mirror a camp. Every guest cottage had its own small boat oared by a servant upon request.

Dinner was served outdoors at a rough-hewn wooden table laden with all kinds of hearty fare. The servants were attentive and Clara and William Lockwood, Jr. were the consummate hosts.

Lily was happy that she could oblige Willy in his quest to please his parents as a suitable gentleman caller. But, she knew his heart was in Africa with the big game he dreamed of rescuing. She also knew her own future was from settled.

She took one look out of the guest room window in the rough and rambling but comfortable camp before she prepared for bed. The moon was shimmering along the waters and a shooting star was darting across the ebon sky.

The breeze blowing in through the open windows was cool and fresh and clear. The lace curtains that hung at the sides of the wooden-framed windows whipped about and the sound of chirping crickets pierced the air. Lily knew she would easily sleep the night away and wake to the sound of birds chirping and fussing about in search of a morning meal.

Chapter Twenty-Seven

L ily stood on the side of a fairly steep hill in the French countryside. A large stone mansion stood behind her at the top and small stone cottages not far below.

The gardens were lovely everywhere and the roses were blooming as well as the daffodils, the iris and the beautiful Gerbera daisies that looked as if they had been painted against the sky. There were cherry blossoms on the dwarf cherry trees behind each cottage and lovely stone chairs set among them. Spring had come to the small town of Aix-de-Provence.

The sun was shining everywhere and made amusing little designs as it playfully went from tree to tree. The soft winds blew through the air and the sky was the bluest Lily had ever seen.

"And, so what do you think?"

"Andre, you startled me. Where is Aggie?"

"She is preparing for tea with Mother. It was kind of you to accompany her. I know John would never let her come without a companion."

"She has been a good friend to me. I so want to repay her for her kindness."

"She has told me how you have supported our friendship. I am grateful, Lily."

"I would not do so unless Aggie was very sure. But, she has assured me of her certainty with the way she admires your generosity in letting her do her causes and not pushing her to be demure and merely a fixture for the benefit of others."

"I would never do that. Aggie has so much to give to the world and I intend to let her. And, she is so much at ease when she is allowed full rein. She has done so much for the Irish and has set out to better their lot. They are making great headway and that child Liam adores her."

"She has invited the heads of the new Chicago labor unions to speak in Boston Commons."

"I will see that she has plenty of protection if that comes to pass. Labor is acting up in France as well and there's no telling what will become of that.

"But, now I must help Father with his new exhibit. He is being threatened by the old guard of artists and almost every art-loving Frenchman in Paris with a riot if he dares to show the works of the new impressionists who have been roundly mocked by the critics. He is concerned for the safety of his gallery.

"The monarchy is on its way out and the nobility must find a way to survive. Father is desperate to save the estate because so many tenant farmers and potteries have been dependent on the House of Boujere for centuries.

"But, I see Aggie is on her way down to see you. I must leave you ladies to chat."

Andre tipped his tweed cap as he strode vigorously up the hill, the morning breeze ruffling his neatly trimmed hair, his walking stick a beautiful turned cherrywood. Aggie stood as she waited for him to approach.

As they stood at the top of the hill, Aggie in a beautiful blue muslin with a parasol to match, Andre in a proper tweed suit, his waistcoat pocket sporting an heirloom watch scrolled with diamonds and rubies and etched with the seal of the House of Boujere, the sun beamed down behind them. As they stood, still in their earnest small talk that only lovers know, they looked to Lily for all they were worth the perfect pair that had graced many an artist's canvas throughout the centuries.

Aggie shaded her forehead as she looked for Lily. "Lily, I have been looking all over for you. You have escaped the morning news and the delightful tea Andre's mother set out on the veranda of the downstairs parlor."

"I thought it perhaps best Madame Boujere get to know you without my interference. And, such a lovely day to contemplate a beautiful view of the countryside."

"That is thoughtful of you, Lily. Andre's mother does not give her approval easily. She is a very stern woman when it comes to this estate which has been in her husband's family for generations. And, she adores Andre who is the sole heir to the House of Boujere."

"Well, she could do no better than the wonderful, caring and kind young lady you have become. But, she must discover that for herself."

"That is very kind of you to say, Lily. Through her stern demeanor it is possible to see a slight spirit of adventure which she seems to have passed down to her son. And, I know she wishes she had been able to support causes beyond this estate but knew she mustn't for it was not the place of a woman to do so.

"I think she sees that in me. And, for that reason if she gives her approval it will be a good alliance.

"But, I must also wait for Mother and Father's approval as well. The Boujere's have invited them to be their guests when they arrive in France. I can only hope for the best.

"Madame Boujere has heard of Mother's avid interest in gardens. She has already prepared cuttings for Mother to take with her when she returns home. I'm sure that will help to soften Mother up. Mother melts at the sight of a beautiful blossom."

"It sounds like Madame has decided to be on your side. You have a very important ally."

"Andre has suggested we go into town and explore the shops and the cafes that line the one street afforded the town. He cautioned they are not like Boston but they might delight us nevertheless with an array of little trinkets to take home."

"That sounds like a wonderful outing."

"Then, we must prepare. Andre has ordered a carriage to take us there. He has also warned that there are occasional rowdies but the shopkeepers and the cafes keep order to protect the reputation of a town that prides itself in respectability."

As Aggie strolled the streets of Aix she seemed very much at home unlike the young lady she was expected to be as the daughter of a family descended from English nobility.

The sun warmed their backs as she and Lily strolled the street of the very small town. A number of townsmen had already sat at the few tables of the outdoor cafes and were raising their glasses of the full-bodied red wines which were typical of the region. There was laughter and camaraderie everywhere.

As they returned to the Boujere estate, the carriage filled with little trinkets, lavender soaps and sachets, and the chocolates of a country that prided itself in the celebration of life the sun sank in a haze of vivid pinks and a rose the likes of which Lily was certain she had never seen. To Lily, travelling in a strange country, it was an omen that bode well for her friend who so desperately wanted to shape her own future and for her own as well.

Chapter Twenty-Eight

L ily looked down on one of the most beautiful views she had ever seen. It was summer in France and despite the heat a lovely summer breeze had come along to cool her off. She felt positively magnificent as she stood at the top of the hill that ran below the Boujere mansion that was the seat of the House of Boujere.

But, as she looked below at the lovely French countryside and the beautiful trees in bloom and the gardens everywhere which looked like one big beautiful canvas waiting to be painted she saw only rough hills and prairies and the crags of mountains in the daylight and their purple hues in the evening. She saw the prairies filled with the vibrant hues of blossoms just burst into bloom ready to pluck, the tall grasses that swayed with the wind, and the Cross Timbers, a haven from the cares of the world, all part of a vast and humbling landscape.

The more civilized world which she had been privileged to be a part of in the past year and a half had tamed the landscape. But, perhaps it was that it had tamed them.

They were filled with proper talk and manners, elegant fashion and sumptuous dinners and rules for just about everything. But, what was left? And, where did she, Lily, fit in?

She had been welcomed into many a noble's parlor in the whirlwind visit with Aggie to introduce her to European society, and was eyed by many a young gentleman as a perfect prospect for courtship, but she feared a life as what she viewed as a trinket.

She saw only a boy, skittish and uneasy at first, who had grown into a strong young man full of the confidence of youth, fishing the waters with ease, bringing down game and providing for a mother he adored. Perhaps it was Wohali who knew her better than she knew herself.

"Have you escaped as well?"

She turned to see John, resplendent in a light linen frock coat, trousers to match and a newly fashionable ascot tie held by a diamond stick pin. "I thought you would be going about your duties as best man."

"Both Aggie and Andre have been so thorough in preparations there is little for me to do. I can only walk about and view the grounds and see much that I would paint in this beautiful landscape.

"But, I am happy for Aggie. When Mother and Father met the Boujeres Mother was certain she would object to the union. To her, the nobles are a dying breed, only after an American heiress's money.

"But, when she toured the gardens with Madame Boujere and saw the blooms Madame had nurtured from seedlings and Father met his match in Monsieur Boujere at chess they were charmed. They gave their blessing and promised to invite our family's noble relations who are highly placed in England and the wealthiest merchants they knew to perhaps take an interest in the Boujere potteries and farmlands."

"Most importantly, Aggie will not be kept down by the unwritten rules of a foolish society. Andre has promised to see to that."

"Yes, and now how about you, Lily? What have you learned from your tour of royal courts and the well-appointed parlors of the nobility?"

"I have found them fascinating. Their graciousness could not be matched and their manners faultless.

"But, they are far removed from the people they are meant to serve. And, far from the new frontier of a hard-scrabble territory where every spade of earth that is turned to plant a seedling represents the hope for a better future.

"But, I fear that I have disappointed Mama. She has groomed me from birth to have the luxuries and reach the heights that she believes she was denied because of her heritage."

"She has given you the opportunity to see the world. But, now you must make your own decisions. You have encouraged me to follow my dream of becoming an artist despite its difficulties and you have encouraged Aggie to stand against society's beliefs that young ladies be mere decorations and speak endlessly of trifles.

"I admire you more than all the young ladies that appear at every ball and grand parties. I have many sketches for which you so kindly sat and I know that someday the paintings they will become will inspire those who take the time to properly view them."

"I am grateful for your many kindnesses, John, and for showing me a world I never would have seen if you had not provided an escort.

"But, now I see we must ready ourselves for the very important roles we will play in such a grand and elegant wedding."

As they walked up the hill the sun rose higher in the sky and the warmth of a hot summer day began to envelop them. They reached the mansion just as a refreshing bowl of strawberry punch laced with the sparkling wine of the lovely Champagne region was set out in the shade of a large old oak and tiny biscuits and small cakes were set about.

The outdoor wedding was scheduled for early afternoon and in the grand ballroom in case of rain. A light summer shower came up but subsided as quickly as it had arrived. The guests proclaimed this a sign of good luck and assembled on the hillside at the appointed hour.

A small orchestra played the works of the great French composers as the guests were seated. John arrived at the makeshift altar covered with blossoms in a black frock coat and trousers to match. He stood as Lily came next. Andre followed, his usual reserved look replaced by one of obvious delight.

Aggie walked with her father as the orchestra broke into the wedding march and several small cousins of both the bride and groom carried her long train. Aggie's gown of yards and yards of Brussels lace and satin and tiny little bows of silver brocade and her long veil of tulle was more beautiful than anything Lily had seen in all of Mama's books.

The wedding reception, where Aggie signed the register, was held in the grand ballroom to save the guests the indignity of swatting small insects that were certain to come out after dark.

A sumptuous supper was served and the guests drank the night away with the best champagne the country had to offer. As the wedding couple departed for a honeymoon which would take them nearly around the world they were pelted with rice and wished the best.

Lily felt alone for the first time in a strange country. She must find John for he and his family would be her escorts home.

As she stood her thoughts nearly drowned out the noise of the gaiety and the revelry and the guests seemed a caricature of the photographs and paintings she had thumbed through for years in Mama's books of the very same scene.

She must find a washroom and tidy up the combs

and flowers she had placed so carefully in the hairdo a French maid had coaxed into the latest French fashion. As she looked through the open unshuttered windows at the summer sky above with stars almost hanging in the ebon stillness she knew the guest room Madame Boujere had so generously set aside for her with the large feather bed would later be a most welcome sight.

Chapter Twenty-Nine

As Lily strolled down New York's Fifth Avenue on the arm of Willy Lockwood III she was entranced by the tall buildings and the crowds of people swarming the city streets bent on getting somewhere only they knew. People rushed about and carefully avoided everyone else in their quest for yet another destination.

Elements of transportation whizzed about everywhere. Trolleys clanged through the streets while elevated trains ran above and hansom cabs were available on every major thoroughfare.

Fall had come to New York but no one seemed to notice. Trees were noticeably absent left out in favor of miles and miles of concrete walkways and buildings that vied for height.

Although Willy's family lived high above Central Park in a beautiful penthouse and owned just about every kind of conveyance for their private transportation Willy had insisted they take a hansom cab to get to their destination so Lily could get the full flavor of a city far removed from the genteel atmosphere of Boston.

Willy had set about to show Lily the highly developed financial district where his father had a suite of well-appointed offices and the cultural and theatrical side of a city obviously different from all others. Lily wondered how anyone got their work done in a place that seemed to be all about elbowing each other out to get to a predetermined destination.

They were headed for luncheon at one of the poshest and most famous restaurants in New York. Delmonico's, famous for originating a potato dish, soups and desserts which spread across the country had been host to the famous from royalty and theater actors to presidents and the most celebrated authors of the day.

Willy took Lily's elbow as he steered her into a corner entrance with heavy double doors half glass flanked by imported Pompeiian pillars with the name of the restaurant spelled out above in simple and elegant gold letters. "We are here. Please ignore the noise. Diners come here to be seen and to chat with their friends and business partners in hopes of a more lucrative day and to assess that very pesky competition that is out to ruin them.

"But, they are also here for the best dining experience in a public restaurant. Even the very critical *New York Times* has claimed its banquet menus "luxurious."

Willy was greeted promptly and ushered to a very special table in the back. "Thank you, Pierre. Please have Gerard bring a copy of the wine list and have him pour us the best champagne you have in the house."

"Right away, Monsieur Lockwood. We have had a new shipment directly from Champagne with some rare sparkling wines that have aged and are known by the best wine critics as the years to uncork.

"Gerard will be over promptly as you request. Meanwhile, please be seated and relax with your very lovely companion. Chef Andre has a special hors d'oeuvre he will send to your table as Gerard pours your wine aperitif.

"Thank you, Pierre. Please bring a menu."

As Willy poured over the menu, a very plain-looking affair with dishes of every kind crammed onto one sheet, a bite-sized hors d'oeuvre was set in front of them, caviar wrapped in a sliver thin slice of smoked salmon along with carrot shavings in a small pool of red pepper sauce and golden raisins. Gerard, a very stately dark-haired man gloved and perfumed with impeccably curled hair who spoke almost no English, stood poised with one hand across his back to steady his stance as he poured slowly a small amount of the chilled champagne into a flute set in front of Willy.

"It's fine, Gerard. As a matter of fact, it's delicious. You must have had to pull some strings to get such a wine directly from Champagne."

"I work very closely with the owners who have ties to just about every winery in Europe. Both Mr. Delmonicos are very particular about their wine lists."

As they sipped champagne Willy looked at Lily. "Lily, you must taste a dish that is served only in this restaurant. The Delmonicos serve a dish of lobster that even your grandmother will not have tasted devised by a former sea captain. Despite the many delicate seafood dishes that kitchen servants and Boston restaurants have mastered this new one is quite delicious.

"Now, tell me what your plans for the future are. I must know for I have missed your company."

"I see you have not changed your bold demeanor from the time we met at Grandmother's ball."

"I see no reason to change it. I am a young man in search of a goal that will satisfy my hunger to stand on my own two feet but contribute to the less fortunate elements of our so-called society.

"I was not born into wealth. Father struck oil when I was about ten. I have not forgotten the struggles Mother and Father hid often from me.

"But, I have not forgotten my desire to save the beautiful beasts that have had to suffer because certain elements of man consider themselves superior to the most beautiful animals on earth.

"I have quietly put out the word that I am looking for a spot on the African continent that would be fertile enough to grow coffee. Next, I must find a way to convince Father to support me in such a business venture."

"Well, I can see you have not given up your lofty goals. I am told that good luck will often come to the most persistent."

"Thank you, Lily. You are so far the only support I have in what most consider a very foolish venture. But, I am not willing to claim defeat."

"From what I have read Africa is a place of sun and simple natives. I'm sure a person with your persistence could do well there."

"And, what are your plans, Lily? If you ever want adventure you will know where to look. You will always be able to find me."

"That's just it. I'm not sure what I want. Since my whole life has been planned from the time I was born I haven't had a chance to think on it."

"I think you will know when the time comes. And, when it does I hope that fortune will favor you. You have been a welcome ally in a wish I have had since my youth and I am truly grateful.

"But, right now we must taste the dish served only at Delmonico's that has sent presidents and the famous alike prattling about the great culinary adventure they experienced in a growing city that not long ago they deemed barely civilized."

As Lily savored the delicate chunks of lobster bathed in a sauce of French cream, butter churned on the dairies of local farmers and laced with the best imported sherry she was certain that every bite carried the creator's passion for the open sea.

The afternoon was filled with exploring the new art museum built at the edge of the magnificent Central Park mostly hung with European treasures. Lily was certain that John's paintings would someday grace its walls.

Lily was overwhelmed with the choices facing New Yorkers. The city had risen from a haven of crime and corruption to fast becoming the cultural center of the nation.

Willy insisted on touring the theater district before her departure. The theaters were lavish and a few lit by the new invention of electricity. She was delighted with the antics of vaudeville and made sure to etch it in her memory so she could describe every song and dance to Mama and Papa.

As Lily returned to Boston with Willy seeing her off at the train station she could not wait to return to what she was certain was the slower pace of a city with far better manners but the excitement of a city that had survived gangs and riots to become a city of dazzling entertainment, exquisite art galleries and home to the most diverse population she had ever seen struggling daily to find common ground would not soon leave her memory.

Chapter Thirty

Lily returned from New York to find Harper Taylor in the parlor of Miss Stanton's School for Girls pacing the floor and looking more distraught than she had ever seen him.

"Lily, Lita has left Boston while I was away making arrangements for a place with the Rothschilds' New York firm. I didn't give her my reasons for travelling there because I wanted it to be a surprise if I was successful."

"It is a shock to me as well. She gave me no warning. I would not have left if I thought she had been in distress."

"If I have hurt her in any way I would want to know and perhaps make amends. But, she gave me no knowledge that she was unhappy."

"Nor me. I never shared with her the unkind remarks I overheard at Grandmother's ball. I wanted the evening to be everything she had wanted it to be."

"I believe it was. But, I suppose it was not possible to ignore the snubs of the matrons as we danced the night away leaving their daughters to search for partners elsewhere."

"You must not blame yourself, Harper. I have not seen Lita so happy as she was that night.

"If you will seat yourself I will find George to bring you a glass of sherry. Perhaps it will settle your nerves while I search for an answer to Lita's hasty departure."

Lily rounded the corner down the long hallway to the small office that housed Miss Stanton's desk and mountains of paperwork that somehow never seemed to diminish. "Come in, Lily. I have been waiting for you. I was unable to reach you in New York and hope you had a pleasant journey."

"I did, Miss Stanton, thank you. But, I am perplexed about Lita. She gave me no indication that she was planning to leave. Did she confide in you her whereabouts or the reason she chose to leave a place where I thought she was very happy?"

"She did not confide her reasons for leaving but she did give me her destination. She has planned to leave the school for a return to her home. She gave me no reason for her departure but to say she had been very happy here and thanked me for the privilege of studying at such a fine institution.

"I tried to persuade her to wait until you returned but she politely refused. It seemed she had made her mind up and anything I could say would not dissuade it.

"Lily, I hope you will unravel this mystery because Carmelita was one of our best students. She was a joy to me as my personal assistant over the summer recess and she never neglected to help a student in need. Her harp playing brought the most heavenly sounds and she was excited to look forward to our annual recital for which she spent hours practicing in earnest."

Miss Stanton reached into her desk drawer and pulled out a lovely cream-colored note with Lily's name scrawled carefully across its sealed envelope. "Carmelita left you a note. I hope it explains her hasty departure.

"I sent Simon who has been with us for many years and is a very trusted servant to accompany her to her destination in Oklahoma. She will be well looked after on her journey."

"Thank you, Miss Stanton. I must look after Mr. Taylor. He is in dire need of consoling at the moment."

"Lily, if you need anything at all please let me know."

"I will, Miss Stanton. Thank you for your concern."

As Lily returned to the parlor she noticed some color had returned to Harper's countenance. She pulled the letter from the envelope and began to read.

My Dearest Cousin,

I am indebted to you for all you have done for me. I do not wish to cause you further harm.

I overheard the most vile gossip from the hushed tones of the kitchen servants as they passed about the dinners last evening while you were gone. It seems the matrons of Boston are planning to confront the Taylors and demand that Harper break his friendship with me or they will take further action. They believe it is causing a stain on the whole of Boston society to bring a person without pedigree into what they claim is the most genteel and well-guarded society of any in the east. They fear they will lose business and the foothold they have had over the other developing cities and ports in the northeast.

I cannot be responsible for the ruination of Harper's future success. Harper has been everything to me and I am not sure how I will live out my life without him. I wish only for him the very best life fortune has in store for him.

Please forgive me for causing you distress.

Your loving cousin,
Carmelita

Harper sat silent. Then, he spoke. "I have just been fortunate to secure a good position with the New York Rothschild's branch if I want it. I have also gotten a promise from Mrs. Blakely Hanford whose husband heads the New York firm and who is very close to all the Rothschild wives that she will be happy to be a patron to Lita. She thinks very highly of Miss Stanton's school and will use all the leverage she has to make Lita happy.

"But, now Lita will never know. The fates have not been very kind to us but I think I am a match for the worst they can devise.

"Lily, I must go after her. I cannot live my life without Lita by my side. But, I fear she might not listen to me. I fear she will think me too forward.

"Lily, you have been a friend to both of us and I am grateful. But, I beg of you one more favor. Would you be kind enough to intercede for me?"

"I will agree only because my cousin's happiness means as much to me as my own. Lita has been selfless as my companion often sacrificing her own comforts for my well-being."

The sun went down as Lily unpacked and the moon came up, a sliver of a new moon with a glow that seemed to shine beyond the universe. The sky was lush with stars, some twinkling, some still, some streaking across the darkened skies in a fiery quest to reach the Earth.

She climbed up into the feather bed, the weariness of travel overcoming her. She laughed as moonbeams crept in through the open window bouncing off the walls and the ceiling and back again making patterns that looked like a rabbit and perhaps a squirrel. She fell asleep despite the clatter of carriage wheels and the clanging of trolleys rising from the streets below.

Chapter Thirty-One

Mama rushed around checking candlesticks and vases. Flowers were everywhere brought in from florists with a knack for wedding décor.

Lily was as enthralled as if she were the bride. Mama had spared no expense.

Harper had come to Oklahoma and had fallen at the feet of a simple country girl and she had accepted his proposal, certain that she would rather take all the cruelty that a vicious society could hand out than live without the young gentleman who had enchanted her with his honesty, his spirit of adventure, his kindness and his outright flaunting of a society that knew no boundaries since they had met.

As for Lita, she had cried herself to sleep every night since her return. Aunt Maria, who was as patient as the milk cows that were stanchioned in their barn, could find no way to console her.

It was Lily who convinced her to trust herself, to put faraway the sounds of the wagging tongues of envy and spite.

But, it was Harper who swept her off her feet. To her he was every bit the prince who rescued the princess in the books Lily had shared with her in childhood.

Mama had hidden her disappointment that the wedding would be Lita's and not Lily's. But, her enthusiasm to show off her gentility and the graciousness she had acquired from the stacks of magazines she sent for overrode that.

Prissy arrived with loads and loads of gifts running from the handsome carriage she arrived in to hug Lily. "You must show me Oklahoma, Lily. Father and Mother were certain I would be eaten by savages before I arrived."

"Then, we have time to explore before we begin the ceremony. With the flurry of preparations we will not be missed."

Prissy turned serious as they stood on a hillside behind the manse. The plains, the grasslands and the prairies stretched before them toward the mountains and the haze of the horizon beyond. An arc of green and yellow, red and violet shown in the sky above them, a gift of a light summer rain.

"I have never seen so much open space. It is so different from the streets of Boston."

"I'm so glad you came, Prissy. Harper wasn't certain if you would think it proper to attend."

"Harper has always been my big brother. He has never failed to see to my comforts.

"I know his reputation among the matrons and how he viewed courtship. But, he was young with an adventurous spirit. He disappointed many a matron but he never harmed any of their daughters most of whom were as bored as he was with the rituals of feigned courtship.

"Lita has brought gaiety and laughter into his life. He has a purpose and I never saw him so determined."

"But, I suppose attending such a wedding will mar your social standing and lose chances for a proper courtship of your own."

"I would not want to keep company with any young gentleman who could not think for himself.

"We are a young country, Lily, and we must make our mark. We cannot be run by outmoded customs that are dying in Europe.

"Mother gave up her dream to become a concert pianist to marry Father. But, I know inside she is yearning for the beautiful music she abandoned."

"Well, we must hurry to change into our gowns. We are an important part of the wedding party and we mustn't be late."

The wedding ceremony was as lovely as it could be out on the back hillside with an arch of flowers under which the bride and groom would exchange their vows. Lita looked beautiful, her hair swept back with a length of curls cascading below, her gown a vision of satin and sprays of flowers, her delicate tulle veil the length of her dress held by a floral crown.

Uncle Luis walked Lita down the aisle and Aunt Maria watched with pride. A trio of violins Mama had sent for played music that seemed to mingle with the soft breezes that wafted about and Daniel, now a hefty three, carried the ring. The rest of the little ones carried Lita's long train jockeying for place.

There were many toasts and much to Mama's discomfort Grandmama treated the wedding guests to a dance she remembered from her childhood spent around many a campfire with Uncle Luis playing along, her skirt of many colors flying about, her tambourine and bangles keeping the rhythm.

"Lily, this has been a beautiful wedding. I know Harper is grateful. But, I also know he keeps his sadness to himself that Mother and Father chose not to attend."

"Perhaps they will see things differently in the future. Time has a way of opening people's eyes."

"I hope that is true. Harper's struggles have been my struggles. We were thrown together as children while Father was busy building a business and Mother was busy throwing parties to impress the wives of the important tycoons who were already successful."

"Your father seems to have an adventurous spirit. He was quite taken with my accounts of the territories. It seems that he has passed that spirit onto his son. And, that spirit binds them even if it is unspoken."

"Your words give me comfort, Lily. But, I must stay strong for Harper. I managed to wrest out of Father some words of good will before I left. I must pass them along to Harper."

As Prissy mingled with the crowd to find Harper, Lita threw her arms around Lily. "Thank you Lily for you and Aunt Elena giving me the wedding I have always dreamed of. I hope I can repay you someday."

"You will repay me only with your happiness. You have a long road ahead and many struggles. But, you are just as much a part of these hills as I am. The days we spent giggling about, sharing our secrets, and giving in to the little ones will carry you through."

"I must go now. Harper has planned an extensive honeymoon to give the matrons of both New York and Boston a chance to get used to the idea. I will purchase the best wardrobe in Europe that I can directly from the houses of Paris to give me an edge.

"But, Harper has other plans, too. He has made contact with some mine owners here in Oklahoma. If they strike oil as they have in some of the nearby territories he will make a fortune for himself and the Rothschilds."

The bridal couple was pelted with wheat from the fields of Oklahoma as they left on their extended honeymoon. The guests departed in a variety of conveyances, among them the most elegant carriages brought by some school chums of Harper's who had sworn in the purity of their youth to stick by each other no matter what befell them.

Lily walked out onto the back hillside. The stars were thick in the sky. She wondered where she belonged in the universe they lay so comfortably in.

She could feel Wohali's presence across the prairies, the grasslands, the meadows, the forests and even the mountains. The night sounds of the coyotes and the bobcats reminded her of the scampering about of the rabbits and the squirrels in the Cross Timbers as they had prepared to share a meal and the stars a reminder of the ones they had wished on together.

She wondered what he was thinking or even if he remembered her at all. She had been gone a long time and to a much different place. Had she changed so much? Had he succumbed to the pleas of the tribal elders to take an Indian maiden for his wife?

She put her thoughts aside as she walked slowly back into the house. Mama would be wanting to crow over her success in throwing a party as elegant as anything in the east. She would be wanting Lily to help sort out the photographs when they arrived to send to Grandmother and to regale her with the gossip she had overheard.

She decided to slip upstairs to her room unnoticed. She wished for Lita's happiness as she brushed her hair the one hundred strokes she had learned at Miss Stanton's. Goodness knows Lita deserved it.

As she pulled the rose-covered quilt up beneath her chin she fell asleep in the very bed that had given her so much childhood comfort.

Chapter Thirty-Two

The sun was high as Lily rode in Papa's new buggy, the top down, the wind flying through her hair as she and Papa headed toward the mines. Papa had taken ill and she had insisted on staying over Mama's protests to help nurse him back to health.

The strong wind was putting a rosiness back in his cheeks as they rode the prairies and the grasslands to the foothills of the mountains. Lily refrained from asking him to stop as she had done so long ago in childhood so she could pick a bouquet for Mama and Cook but she reveled in the scent of the newly sprung orchids, the wild roses and the lilies rising from the prairies as they rode through.

As they reached the mines Jamie was there to greet them. "Good mornin' Mr. P. Pa sent me to take care of the men today. He's feelin' poorly."

"Thank you, Jamie. I'm glad to see you."

Jamie reached for Lily to help her down. "Why, Lily, it's nice to see you. We've missed you around here."

Lily headed for the station house, its ramshackle appearance unchanged. She pulled the inkpots from their shelves and set up the books. It had been long since she had added figures or even thought about business. But, she was determined to help Papa.

As she sat, musing out the window toward the trees of the mountain below, Jamie stuck his head in. "I had no notice of you coming, Lily. But, would you care to share my midday meal? It's not much but I think it would do."

"I'd be delighted, Jamie. Let me know when the whistle blows."

As Lily followed Jamie down the long steep path of the mountain below to look for the perfect picnic spot she looked around at the trees, the sturdy oaks, the redcedars and the tall green pines all vying for space. She looked at Jamie leading the way. He looked taller than she had remembered but more filled out. "It looks like farming agrees with you."

"It's hard work but honest work. I plan to make something out of it. But, it takes time.

"And you, Lily. You've changed. You're all grown up."

"I have lived the life of the rich and learned their manners and dances. I've learned to sew a fine stich and to play a fine tune. I have learned what to say and what not to say and how to say it.

"I'm surprised some earl hasn't taken you for his bride. I thought that your Mama had set her sights on that."

"I could never learn to be a part of that world. They have tamed the landscape and call it civilization. But, you can never tame nature.

"But, I'm afraid I am a disappointment to Mama. She has wanted for me what she never could have."

"Well, you're still the most beautiful girl in Oklahoma. And, the smartest.

"You shoulda heard Mr. P. brag about you. He would spout all the places you've been with the pride of a proud papa. But, I know he missed you, Lily. It's pretty plain he has set his sights on you.

"As for me, I've had to help Pa out here at the mines as well as take over the fields.

"Abby's married now and expectin'. Her Jessie is a real good farmer and can provide for them already. But, Ma insisted Samantha and her beau wait until he could provide for them both.

"He's eyein' the fields now that he sees Jessie and the bumper crops he harvested last year. I think I can turn him into a farmer yet."

"Well, your family's lucky to have you."

"They've been pretty good to me. Ma's always put extra leather she's tanned herself to give strength to the jackets she turns out for me and I know she always gave me an extra helping at supper when the crops were good.

"As for Pa, he's been pretty easy going. He says I can take over the farm if I want to but he says if I want to set out for other parts of the world I have his blessing."

"What about you, Lily. Will you be going back east?"

"I'm not sure. Grandmother's waiting for word. But, Papa needs me here."

"I'm not one to give advice, but I know you know yourself. You've never backed down since I laid eyes on you the first day you came here with Mr. P. You were the only girl who could beat me at marbles and the only one who didn't give up when tromping the woods to find a baby nestling or tracking a rabbit to its home when it scampers about."

"Will you be taking off for other parts of the world?"

"I couldn't leave Ma and Pa. Pa's getting on and Ma tires easy.

"But, I love farming. There's nothing like getting up in the morning before the rooster crows and watching the sun come up and dry off the morning dew. And, walking behind the plow and turning up the first earth of spring. There's so much hope in that.

"We'd better get back. Mr. P. likes the men down in the mines in time for the afternoon shift. He's onto something but he never lets on. He doesn't like to give the men too much hope in case he's wrong. He says it dashes their spirit."

"Papa thinks a lot of them. They've been with him a long time. He says if it wasn't for their hard work Mama wouldn't have what she wants and Oklahoma would be just a dried up old territory with nothing in it."

Jamie packed up the scraps of their noonday meal and placed them in his pack as they strolled back up the mountain, the well-worn path full of the pebbles the squirrels and the rabbits scattered about. The deep green leaves of the oaks and the elms sparkled in the early afternoon sun and the birds chirped loudly as they picked at the small red and purple fruit of the hackberry tree.

Neither spoke as they parted at the top, Lily headed for the station house and Jamie for the mines. Lily mused as she looked at the stacks of books in front of her. Jamie was as uncomplicated as the day was long. The happy boy who had grown into this happy man was as certain of his future as he was that the stars would come out at night.

She turned to the books and attempted to make them balance. As the afternoon sun found its way through the station house windows despite their hazy appearance, she filled the inkpots and set to work.

Chapter Thirty-Three

L ily looked over the trees leafed out in their best summer greenery and the prairies rife with wildflowers as she guided the horses of the open two-seater she had elected to use toward Grandmama's. The two-seater was filled with gifts Mama had purchased for the winter.

She was excited to make the trip herself since she mostly saw Grandmama on holidays when she was busy or on rare occasions when Mama had gotten her something special. She was hoping that Grandmama would ask her riddles or at the very least tell her the tales of her gypsy ancestors which used to delight her so much in childhood.

But, she knew she must act more grown-up and very refined because Mama had been regaling her with stories of the grand balls she had attended and the invitations she had received for gatherings in the posh drawing rooms of European nobles.

Lily sighed as she remembered the childish pleasures she had had at Grandmama's knee and the delight her wild dancing to the tune of a gypsy fiddle, its music full of joy and visions of freedom of a people forced to wander had given her.

She slowed as she neared the small cabin. Uncle Mario, who had already hitched up his wagon for a trip to town to purchase supplies, was there to greet her, along with Grandmama and he was happy to give her the big bear hug he usually reserved for her. He teased that she had grown up without his permission and led the horses to the big barn behind the cabin.

Uncle Mario had never married but was content to stay in the small cabin with Grandmama and live his life out taking care of the woman who had raised her children with love despite the loss of her husband at so early an age. He went to town from time to time to visit with a variety of women but none of them tickled his fancy enough to settle down. But, he had many men friends he could beat at poker and drink an occasional mug of ale with and smoke a good cigar when any of them came across a box just in from the east that the owner of the general store would save for them.

Grandmama rushed from the cabin, her large hoop earrings glistening in the sun. She wrapped her arms around Lily with such joy, ushering her in through the

284

open doorway as she spoke. "Lily, what a nice surprise. How nice of your Mama to send you."

She stood back to survey Lily. "My how you have changed. You have become such a fine lady. Your Mama must be very proud.

"We must go to the barn and see the new baby lamb that was born yesterday. I will name her Lily in honor of your visit."

Grandmama stepped lively as they made their way to the barn, her long silver hair tied back with a simple red bow. The fields lay to the left, lush with crops. "We must be quiet. The new ones need their rest."

As they entered, the baby lamb was suckling, barely able to stand on its feet, the mother ewe standing patiently to feed her new charge. "Now, you have a namesake. She is beautiful just like you, Lily. She will give us much wool when she grows to full size."

Grandmama waited to close the barn door until the lamb was finished and lay down to rest. "You must see what Uncle Mario has grown. We must pick some beans and tomatoes and summer squash for you to take home for your supper. And, the sunflowers grow tall this time of year.

"But, first we must go in and drink some tea. I have

some leaves of the elder flower and the peppermint plant. We will brew the leaves while you tell me all about the east and what you have learned."

Grandmama boiled water on the large iron stovetop while Lily settled herself at the large oak table with the checkered tablecloth Grandmama had admired on one of her infrequent trips to town. Then, she pulled her prized crockery teapot, its lid chipped but its reds and blues still as bright as the day they were painted out of the cupboard above. "I have been saving these leaves for a very special occasion. We will steep them and then see what they will tell us."

"Now, Lily, you must tell me what those drawing rooms of the nobles were like. They must have been so grand."

"They were, Grandmama. But, they were filled with people who knew only idleness and mindless chatter."

"My people were chased away from their towns and their cities and forced to wander. But, the fiddle playing and the dancing drew them to our campfires at night. They believed we had magical powers and I saw many a noble with his lady dressed in fine clothes drop shiny gold coins at our feet to get their fortunes told."

"Grandmama, what was Grandpapa like?"

"He was big and strong. He had thick dark hair and deep brown eyes that flashed when he played the fiddle as I danced."

"We were from two different tribes and we met by chance when we were both ten when our tribes were camped along the same beach but Grandpapa never lost track. He said I had stolen his heart and we must never part.

"When we were sixteen Grandpapa proposed that we run away to America where we could lead a more settled life.

"Life was hard at first but we worked together and the first crop we grew here in the territories fed our growing family. When we lost him to the twister I didn't think I could go on but his sons who were the spitting image of him planted the seed, plowed the fields, and reaped plenty a fall bounty from their hard work."

"But, your Mama who was the oldest never got over the loss of her doting papa who never forgot to carve her a trinket in his spare time. She never got over the taunts of the townspeople who teased her mercilessly because we were so poor."

"Now, we have finished our tea and we must read our tea leaves. My own grandmama was an expert fortune teller and when I was barely more than a babe she put me at her side to learn the secrets of what many were certain were her magical powers."

"Lily, your tea leaves are scattered. Happiness will come your way but it may come when you least expect it. You must embrace it for happiness is often fleeting.

"Now, we must tidy up and send you home. Your Mama will be waiting."

Uncle Mario returned to hitch up the buggy and pack it full of enough summer squash, beans and tomatoes to send Cook into the kitchen to devise new recipes and Mama to oversee them.

The sun was setting and the clear, cloudless blue of the sky was painted with swatches of the most beautiful oranges, pinks, reds and violets. Lily admired the canvas vast above the mountains as she crossed the prairies. The moon would soon rise and the stars along with it.

She hurried the horses. Mama would be waiting to hear the latest news.

Chapter Thirty-Four

Lily looked out the window as she rose with the dawn. The day looked bright and sunny and she was determined to make the most of it.

It had been long since she had visited the Cross Timbers, the woods that had given her so much comfort in what was often a lonely childhood. She dressed practically in a pair of riding breeches, a simple shirtwaist, and tied her hair back with a single bow, its deep blue the color of the sky on a windy day.

She chose a mount that was young and frisky and set off across the plains and grasslands. The late summer daisies, risen as white and pure as the winter snow that covered the vast landscape ran across the meadows, along with the deep purple of the prairie violet and the bands of yellow asters.

The day was slightly breezy and the gentle gusts of wind tossed the stallion's mane about as the squirrels and the rabbits hastened to scamper out of his path, the bees buzzed as they searched for the sweetest blossoms newly risen, and the birds flying across the grasslands in search of food chirped an early morning greeting.

As they reached the Cross Timbers Lily tied the mount to a sturdy oak, drawing water from the nearby stream to cool him off. She exchanged her boots for the moccasins she had packed away so long ago and walked the narrow path that took her deep into the woods that gave nurture to the gnarly oaks that had stood for hundreds of years, the tangles of vines crawling their trunks snagging her clothes as she went.

As she rounded the corner she saw Wohali placing the game he had taken down in his pack. "Why, Lily, you have come back. William tried to tell me that I must take a Cherokee woman before I insulted the offerings of the tribe.

"But, I told him I could not. I must wait.

"I pray to the Great Spirit every day for your safe return. But, I know that if his great being finds he cannot grant my wish you will be with me always. For among these trees I can see no one but you.

Lily stood, staring at the youth she had left who had become a man. Wohali looked every bit the picture of the many braves who had come before him.

"Come, we must walk to the waters as we once did.

The summer brings many fat fish to the stream that runs alongside.

The sun was high and the cloudless sky a beautiful blue. As Wohali led along the narrow path and reached for her hand to keep her from the rushing waters below it was as if they had never let go the clasp that had bound them together so long ago.

Lily sat as Wohali waded the stream, his shirt on the grassy bank beside her, the layers of gray shale rising behind them, tree roots sprouting tiny new leaves poking out from the dirt settled between them as he pulled fish after fish into his pack. Then, he pulled himself up to sit on the bank beside her.

"We must stroll to the clearing ahead. The waterfall of the mountain is full of the waters of the heavy rains that settle at its top in the lake above it. As it falls it is the color of all the rainbows in the sunlight.

"You must tell me what you saw in the east. But for the buffalo hunt I have never been far from the small cabin my father built."

"I saw cities full of people. I saw big buildings. I saw people rushing everywhere.

"But, I missed the trees and the hills and the mountains that somehow seem to speak to you."

"Someday, my people will be forced to live like that as well. The Europeans come and they push us farther and farther away.

"My father only desired peace, not war and for that he was run off the tribal grounds of his birth.

"My friend Ahuli is chief now and he says we must fight with treaties, not war. He has asked for my help.

"I have helped William build a trading post. Now, he no longer has to travel.

"Our trading post is very busy. The nearest post is more than a day's journey away and those who come like William because they believe him to be fair.

"Indians of all tribes come to us and the new settlers from the east as well. There they must be patient and understand each other.

"Lily, I have thought only of you these past years while you've been gone. I have missed you because I have known that no matter where you were you were as much a part of these hills as I am.

"I know I have no right to ask you to be my woman. I cannot offer you what the white man can.

"But, I ask because when I first saw you in the forest where I came every day to bring down game you offered to share your meal with me. I thought you the most beautiful creature I had ever seen. I knew then that I would someday ask you to be my woman.

"The sun goes down as we speak and the colors of the waters rushing down the mountainside go with it."

A cool breeze came up and Wohali pulled a light jacket from his pack and placed it around her shoulders and held her to keep her from the chill.

As they stood watching the moon come up over a beautiful sunset of pinks and oranges they were almost a silhouette of two people humbled by a vast landscape that almost bespoke the future.

Lily untied the stallion from the oak as she prepared to ride for home. The sky was dark and filled with stars but the full moon that shone upon the grasslands and the prairies lit the way.

Chapter Thirty-Five

L ily stood on Cherokee tribal grounds in a tear dress, a simple red flounced cotton with colorful bands of triangles and squares scattered about, the dress of ancient Cherokee rites that Ahyoka had sewn. Wohali stood beside her in a ribbon shirt, traditional garb as well.

They were being joined in an ancient Cherokee rite despite Mama's objections.

They exchanged a piece of deer meat and an ear of corn to symbolize the hunt and the hearth and honored the three forces of nature, wind, fire and water. They drank from a two-spouted vessel to symbolize harmony and were blessed by the holy elder.

The tribe celebrated for hours with songs and dances and food and drink. Ahyoka had brought some delicate tea cakes with honey and sesame and William had come in his very best attire, leather breeches, a white shirt and string tie.

Ahuli extended his hand in welcome. "Welcome, Lily. I wish you and Wohali much happiness. Wohali and I were boyhood friends. We often rode our ponies into the far grasslands and took down birds and squirrels and waded the waters for fish and laughed and laughed as they got away from our young hands.

"We were separated when our fathers had their differences. But, I am chief now that my father has passed on and I believe we must move with the times."

The trading post was prospering and Wohali's knack for horse trading brought in traders from near and far. Traders came to seek his opinion and he was able to provide more comforts for Ahyoka. Travelers stopped by in search of shelter and were taken by the totems he carved at night and were eager to make a trade.

As the celebrants were lost in song and dance and joyous revelry they made a quiet departure. Wohali slowed his stallion to a trot as Lily rode alongside.

"My mother prepares a feast for us and William will be there. He brings us an Arab horse as a gift.

"Arabs are the fastest and smartest horses there are and they can run the longest. They have been mounts in war and peace. They are prized by all horse owners.

"But, now we must hurry our mounts. The sun goes

295

down and I must chop more wood for the stove and draw water from the well before the moon rises and the stars fill the skies.

The sun set with large pink swatches across the blue of the sky and the grey haze of twilight arose to gradually turn day into night. The stars and the moon had not yet risen.

As they rode over the last hill that led to Ahyoka's cabin they could see the lights of candles burning brightly inside. Waya came to greet them, barking loudly and spooking Lily's mount. "Waya, you are too loud. You will chase all the rabbits from their holes and they will run away and you will have no meal for tomorrow." Waya wagged his tail nevertheless and followed Wohali to the barn as he bedded the horses down for the night.

Ahyoka came through the door and put her arms around Lily. "I welcome you as my daughter. Now, we must prepare the feast."

At that, William arrived with the chestnut Arab. Wohali came from the barn and marveled at its beauty. It stood proud and erect, several hands high, one of the most beautiful horses Lily had ever seen.

Wohali brushed and groomed the Arab as Ahyoka began to prepare the feast. "I will show you the ways of Cherokee cooking as my mother showed me."

William and Wohali put the fish Ahyoka had cleaned on a stick and cooked it over an open fire. The aroma wafted through the open door as Ahyoka busied herself with stirring the vegetable stew and showing Lily the ways of making hickory nut balls pounded on a hollowed out log and dipped into honey. The aroma of the fish carried on the evening breeze, crickets chirping through the still night air, brought visions of the mountains at twilight and the fresh streams that ran alongside them, their fresh, cool waters ready to quench the thirst of a weary traveler or passer-by.

Ahyoka handed Lily many dishes filled with the delicacies passed down from the ancients to set out on the old pinewood table, chestnut bread, bean cakes, small cakes of blueberry and honey. The chill of the evening air filled the room through the open windows.

William broke the silence. "You must name your Arab."

"I will name him my father's name. He will be Kanuna."

As William left for his cabin, the sun long gone down, Wohali led Lily outdoors. "Tonight we will sleep under the stars. I have prepared a place a short distance from here. It is a clearing where I have spent many hours."

As they walked through the tall grasses, the moon lighting their way as they went, Wohali reached for her hand as he had so long ago along the steep ravine to keep her from the rushing waters below. Moonbeams danced about and the stars shined brightly in the quiet of a clear dark sky. Only the occasional hoot of an owl or a nighttime critter scampering about underfoot broke the silence.

As they reached the clearing a lean to stood out in the moonlight, sprigs of pine and laurel strewn about, totems of good luck and courage among them. They sat, breathing in the fresh crisp air, content in the quiet and peace of a still, dark night.

"My father set aside many acres for the time I would take a woman. Many hills to find wild berries and many fields to hoe and plant.

"Ahuli has offered a place along the river on tribal lands. He has asked me to be part of the tribal council.

"I will join the council to carry on my father's work. The white man's government will soon open these territories to settlers. The rush has already begun.

"The settlers who come before the opening are here to claim the best lands before the others. Many don't live by any laws and think they can take what they want. They come into the trading post drunk with their own homemade ales and William has to settle them down.

"They will want to push my people off their lands or push them farther north. We must trade for better conditions.

"But, you and I, Lily, we must live here. These hills and grasslands are our future.

"The Cherokee must not live in the past. But, they must not forget it for it is the past that gives them strength.

"If I have a son I will teach him as my father taught me. But, I will teach him the ways of the white man as William taught me."

"Wohali, you have been a good son. If your father was here he would be proud."

"He is here. His spirit surrounds us."

As they lay beneath the stars they counted the ones that were still and wished on the ones that twinkled. They laughed and laughed as one streaked across the sky disturbing their count.

Wohali held her to keep her from the chill of the evening. The stars looked brighter than ever before and the moon more peaceful. She was certain the strength she felt as he wrapped his arms around her was the strength that would carry them into the future.

Chapter Thirty-Six

L ily sat astride a beautiful roan, one of Wohali's best trades, as she made her way toward Papa's mines. Though it had been merely a day since their joining everything seemed to be reborn. The trees looked leafier, the grasses greener and more golden, and the sky a more beautiful blue.

Papa had recovered from his illness but his step was slower and his face more worn. She must remember to come more often to help with the books and work on getting shipments of ore to the east by rail.

She must write Grandmother of Papa's recovery and include a prairie wildflower for Grandmother's growing dried flower collection. Grandmother was a trendsetter and Lily was certain that she would be the envy of the garden club with dried blossoms from all corners of the Earth.

When she arrived, Hector was giving the morning instructions to the miners before they went down into the shafts and Papa was bent over the books. "Lily, we have sent many tons of ore east. It will be turned into stones in Boston and shipped to the best designers in Paris and Vienna.

"The miners have come across a lode of the highest quality sapphires and our rubies are close to perfect. They will be heated and polished in Boston and shipped to designers in France and Vienna.

"We almost lost trade when colorful gems went out of fashion during the English queen's period of mourning but it's rising again and even finding new and more ambitious designers.

"There's a new young designer in Paris who's making a name for himself, René Lalique. I have sent him some samples of our rubies and if he agrees to take our stones our corundum will be turned into the finest jewelry sought after by the duchesses and countesses and even the courts of Europe.

At that, Hector stuck his head in. "We're off to a good start, Mr. P. The rocks are giving the boys a hard time but they're determined to pull them loose. By next week we should have a good bunch to ship east."

"Great job, Hector. When's the missus going to stop working so hard?"

"When she stops sewing for the little ones. My Abby's expectin' and she's sewing a whole pile before the little shaver gets here."

"Well, I put a little something in your pay envelope. So, you get her some trinket when you get to the general store."

"Thanks, Mr. P. I know she'll be grateful. She wears herself out minding that brood but she says they're our future and we better mind 'em good.

"Nice to see you, Miss Lily. My Jamie would say hello if he was here."

"Thanks, Hector. It's nice to see you out."

As the early afternoon sun lowered in the sky Lily saddled up the roan and headed for Ahyoka's cabin. She must help Ahyoka with supper and when the dishes were put away and Wohali had chopped the wood and drawn the water they would walk to the hill together to plan their house. Wohali had already piled the logs and had made many good trades to fill a room with a beautiful oak table, some piney chairs and a big sitting chair for the corner.

As she neared the cabin, storm clouds broke up above sending down a heavy rain. William stood in the doorway, leaning on a shovel, his eyes dazed, his face a picture of grief.

"Lily, you must sit. A few days ago some settlers came to Ahyoka's cabin and tried to run her off of her land. She refused to go.

"Today, they broke in and attacked her. Waya was no match for the likes of that Miller gang and he lay beside her. They took everything they could and left the word "Injun" smeared on every wall.

"Wohali returned this morning to look over his trade horses and found them both. He came on the Arab to the post crazed and looking for the best Winchester we had. I told him to wait for the circuit judge and let the law take care of it but he said he couldn't wait, he knew it was those Miller brothers who were breaking the law claiming lands that weren't theirs and he was going to get them.

"I came here to take care of Ahyoka. I placed her next to Kanuna and Waya with her.

"The Arab returned without Wohali and I went to track his path. They had ambushed him at the pass before their cabin and had strung him up before he could fire a shot.

"I have buried him next to Kanuna. The Cherokee believe they will meet in the land of the Divine Spirits."

Lily stared ahead unable to speak. She walked slowly to the meadow beyond and plucked two blossoms and placed them on the two graves. She kneeled at Wohali's. "I will remember the pledge I made to you as I stood beside you before the tribal elder. I will keep it always."

As she rose, her soft tears mingled with the heavy rains. The storm lifted and the sun sank into the grey haze of the western skies.

Chapter Thirty-Seven

Lily surveyed the fields from the veranda of the rambling log farmhouse as they sprouted the early crops of spring. Beans and corn, squash and tomatoes, cucumbers and peppers gave hope to a plentiful late summer and early fall bounty.

The years had turned into a new millennium and the 1900s showed lots of promise for the future. She shaded her forehead against the lowering rays of the afternoon sun as she mused.

Jamie had come to her at the mines as she worked over the books for Papa and quietly mourned for Wohali as she discovered she carried his child. He seemed shy and nervous as he spoke.

"Lily, I would like to make you my wife if you would have me. I don't have as much as the boys in the east but I am a hard worker and I know if we work together we can make something of a farm.

"Pa has given me several acres and I will build you a house you can be proud of.

"I will give your child a home and raise it as my own.

"I have always thought you the most beautiful girl in Oklahoma. I know I will never be able to fill your heart and I know it is reserved for another but if I can have one small corner of it I will work to make you a good husband.

They were married quietly by the circuit judge and settled in the house Jamie built, a sturdy log cabin affair with a veranda and a rocker for Lily to rock the baby to sleep.

Their brood had grown in the following years and now numbered two boys and three girls who eagerly helped their Pa on the farm and together they put in new crops and the fields grew lush under their hands.

She shooed the dogs away from the veranda lest they get underfoot while she drew water from the well. She had planned a big stew for supper and she must start it early so it could simmer on the back burner while she taught the children their lessons.

She called them in from the fields with the large bell that hung from the front post of the veranda. The dogs raced to meet them, barking a greeting as they went.

She stirred the stew as they settled around the large oak table and pulled out their books. Then, she sat, surveying the table. Mary the youngest sat next to

Adahi who she adored and followed around everywhere. Next came Rachel, dimples and saucy black curls, and Amanda, the middle child, soft brown hair pulled back in a ponytail much like Lily had worn when as a child she rode her pony about the prairies filled with wildflowers and the long grasses swaying with the wind. Ephrem, who would rather be out in the fields sowing corn or wheat, sat silently.

Lily held court for most of the afternoon. She must prepare the children for this new century. Things were changing quickly. New colleges were springing up in the east and farming was changing rapidly.

Horseless tractors were being turned out as fast as they could sell and Jamie was fiddling with a new invention that would revolutionize farming if only the companies in the east would show an interest.

She took her apron off and went outside to survey the vista. Hills in the distance and mountains looming behind them. A beautiful prairie to the east with a blanket of wildflowers, the asters and the wild roses, the soft lilac of the prairie violet, and the pale yellow of the tiny buttercup.

The Cross Timbers were not in view but they were in her memory. Not far from here, they stood firm, roots planted in the ground centuries ago, deprived of moisture and hit by ice storms and tornados, their leafy tops shading the forest floor, a place to dream.

The century was moving too fast for her. Towns and villages were springing up where grasslands once were. The railroads had come through the territories and the unassigned lands were filled with settlers who didn't know the first thing about farming and many gave up and turned back.

Her years in the east were just a dim memory save for the few letters and occasional photos she had had from John and Aggie. John had moved to Paris and Aggie was raising a brood of young boys who would inherit an estate bent on saving a dying nobility but was active in the French unions of the future. Willie had sent her one of the first coffee beans grown on the plantation he built with his determination and hard labor.

She shaded her eyes as she looked east. She wasn't certain where she fit in this century that moved with the fastest pace she had seen. She longed for the days of riding the open prairies with the sun at her back and watching the rushing waters of the springs that ran down the mountains glistening in the sun and reflecting the blues and greens of the grasslands.

She must get back to the kitchen and prepare the stew. The children must be fed and there must be time left for sitting around the campfire Jamie often built in the evenings after the chores were done. Adahi played the harmonica and Ephrem kept the beat with two spoons and a stick. Mary danced the dance of her gypsy ancestors that she had begged Grandmama to teach her.

When the children were bedded down and the chores were done Lily changed into her best calico and climbed the hill behind the house. She climbed to the top and waited for a shooting star or a twinkling one.

She spoke to Wohali when the time was right. She was known among some in the town as the crazy lady who spoke to the stars or maybe even, as some might gossip, who bayed at the moon.

"Wohali, I know you are there. I know your spirit watches over us.

"Your son Adahi grows big and strong. He looks as you looked in the prime of your new youth.

"I send him to Ahuli to learn the language of his forefathers. Ahuli says he is doing fine and will soon be able to join the council when he is of age.

"Ahuli says you would be very proud."

She turned and walked down the hill, her buttonhook shoes finding a careful path as she went. The stars were out and the new moon rose behind her as she walked. The scent of pine drifted on the night air from the piney woods behind. The crickets chirped in the brisk night air and a few small critters scampered about.

She went into the house as quietly as she could. Jamie was asleep in the big chair, his pipe unlit lay beside him. She tiptoed to the chest in the corner and lay a quilt over him to keep him from the chill of the night spring air.

She went quietly to the bedroom with the big oak bed and donned a muslin nightgown trimmed with tiny roses. She climbed up on the bed and pulled the comforter over her. She must sleep for the morning came soon and the rooster crowed early as the dew moistened the tall grasses and the fields beyond. There were cows to milk and chickens to feed.

She lay looking out the window into the night air. The sliver of a moon glimmered as it shone against a deep dark sky and the stars twinkled brightly around it.

Endnote

Lily's progeny were many from her marriage to Jamie. She raised Wohali's son Adahi to know his heritage and when he reached legal age he changed his name to Michael and ran for the US Congress to fight for the rights of his people.

Lily and Adahi are fictional but their real life counterparts have distinguished themselves as heads of the Bureau of Indian Affairs and representatives of their native tribes to the United States Senate and House of Representatives.

No longer did the Cherokee attack innocent settlers or take them captive or fight the militia of what could only be called an oppressor's army. Instead they became officers of the Bureau of Indian Affairs and ran for Congress and won.

Like peoples everywhere who have been robbed of their freedom, their heritage remains alive in museums and Native American centers. But, buffalo hunting on the open prairies, planting maize and beans on lands they chose, and moving on to find better hunting grounds as their ancestors before them continues to define their dreams.

Oklahoma

Oklahoma Territory was a rough land filled with a sparse, diverse population. Its natural resources were as diverse as its settlers.

Oklahoma Territory was home to many Native American tribes who fought each other, refused to accept the Native American immigrants from the Trail of Tears, the cruel forced march tearing integrated Native Americans from their comfortable homes in the south by order of President Andrew Jackson to push them farther west, and who were brutally divided on whether or not to cooperate or fight the relatively new United States government that was bent on taking away their lands in favor of white settlers pushing west.

It was filled with Civil War veterans, both Native American and white settlers, who had fought on both sides and had yet to bury their grievances against each other despite the end of the war.

But, it was also filled with a plethora of natural bounty. Oklahoma is home to a wealth of natural resources in a variety of coal mines, oil, and lodes of corundum that are made into precious gems. It also is home to more varieties of birds, flowers and trees than any other state of the Union. Its rough terrain sports a diverse set of natural wonders in the Great Plains, prairies and grasslands, mountains and vast forests, especially the rare and unusual Cross Timbers.

It is most likely that the Cross Timbers reflect best the history of Oklahoma. Filled with hundreds of short, stubby, rough-barked and drought-stressed post and blackjack oaks surrounded by briars, vines and tangles, their treetops branched out so close together they deprive the entire forest of sunlight. But, these four hundred-year-old trees have survived the harshest weather nature has bestowed on Oklahoma, strong winds, frequent ice storms, hail and drought, and tornadoes that arise without warning. As a long-time 1800s Oklahoma rancher described it, "Them old post oaks on the ridges are tough as nails."

It is hard to find an Oklahoma resident or former resident who doesn't speak with the greatest of pride of their home state. But, it is thanks to the men and women who came before them who stayed the course in an unforgiving land, learning to get along with each other and the land they relied on. In 1907 the Oklahoma Territory became the 46th state admitted into the union that is the United States of America.

Discussion Questions

1. Lily is an independent child early on. What factors contribute to her independence? How does she show her independence?

2. As an only child Lily is often lonely. What does she most often do to fill those lonely hours?

3. Lily spends much of her early childhood in the Cross Timbers, a rare ancient forest indigenous to Oklahoma. What are the drawbacks of such an unusual forest? What are the benefits as described by the author? Can you add some benefits of your own? How does spending so many hours among these ancient trees impact Lily?

4. Wohali, the Native American boy Lily meets in the Cross Timbers, is a complex character. Up until their meeting Lily only knows of Native Americans through seeing them as workers at her father's mines and hearing about them as employees from her father. How does she perceive Wohali when they first meet?

5. Wohali and Lily are raised in completely different cultures. What are some of the differences

between the two? What are some of the similarities?

6. How did Lily and Wohali bridge the gap of their two different cultures?

7. Lily also makes friends with Jamie, her father's mine foreman's son, a boy who is somewhat older than she. What is their friendship like?

8. Carmelita, known as Lita, is not only Lily's cousin, she is Lily's best friend. They are opposites in nature. What draws them together?

9. When Lily arrives in Boston, what are some of the contrasts she sees to the territory she grew up in? How does she respond to these contrasts?

10. Lily is a good student at Miss Stanford's school and fits well into Boston society and its manners. But, what are her own thoughts about a society so different from the one she grew up in? How do her thoughts differ from Lita's?

11. How does Lily respond to the relationship between Lita and Harper?

12. Lily makes friends with a number of socialites her own age. How does she respond to them?

13. Although Lily has many offers of courtship she finds none that appeal to her for marriage. What stands in her way?

14. Do you think the story that Lily's grandmother tells Lily of why her father left his family and its wealth so abruptly to strike out on his own impacts her?

15. How do the natural environments of Oklahoma and Boston and the attitudes of their settlers toward them affect the societies they both become? How do the two societies differ in their approach to their natural surroundings? How do you think your own natural surroundings have affected you?

16. In what ways does Lily represent the courage of those who settled the west? How would you have approached the life of a settler in the early days of this country's rugged territories?

Conversation with Jan Surasky

What inspired you to write *The Sound of Unheard Melodies?*

I had very much enjoyed writing the stories of the main character's ancestors in my previous novel *The Lilac Bush Is Blooming* that were woven throughout the main story. One of my favorites was the one about an Indian maiden who danced wildly among the hilltops and was the child of an Indian chief's daughter and a white trader. I wanted to do something with that and perhaps expand it but instead I began to think about a Native American boy who had been a high school classmate and had been so tormented as he lived between two societies that he eventually took his own life. I knew I had to memorialize his tragedy somehow and give back what his friendship had meant to all my classmates. So, I set about to tell the story of the Native Americans at the time European settlers began to arrive and eventually to encroach on what had been their territories.

Why did you choose to set it in Oklahoma?

As I did research on the country's Native American tribes I found them most prevalent in what is now Oklahoma when they were pushed west by the new United States government.

What was it like to do research on Oklahoma?

It was all new information to me. I knew nothing about Oklahoma. The more I researched the more fascinated I became with its history and its riches. When it came time to move the main character to Boston I had so enjoyed writing about Oklahoma I didn't want her to go.

What was it like to research Boston?

I knew slightly more about Boston than Oklahoma. I had visited it a number of years ago and was somewhat more familiar with it. Boston has a rich history as well as one of our earliest settlements. It also had a diverse population as did Oklahoma making it a perfect place to juxtapose against the diverse population of Oklahoma. Also the heavy influence of Europe on Boston society and the lack of it in the western territory of Oklahoma made it a good contrast.

How did the novel come to be about Oklahoma when you set out to tell the story of Native American struggles at the outset of this new government?

As I researched Oklahoma and became more fascinated by its history and many natural resources the story that I had set out to write as a general theme became more and more eclipsed and it somehow became the story of Oklahoma.

What was it like to research Cherokee and gypsy culture and history which played a large part in the lives of your characters?

It was so very enjoyable and educational. I was so moved and entranced by the reminiscences of both the Romani people, commonly known as gypsies, and of the Cherokee who have posted and written about their respective heritages and have passed along the traditions in rites, dress and wonderful cookery with such pride.

Do you outline your novels before you write?

I do not outline or have any written notes. When I get an idea I let it simmer first and then I know the first sentence and I know how the book will end. I know the main character and perhaps another main character or two and I know the setting. I know vaguely some of the things that will take place. And, with that I set out to tell their story. But, I am just as surprised as the reader as to what will happen next or what characters or sub characters will enter the novel.

What was the most challenging part of writing this book?

As with all my novels getting the characters right. After all, they alone give voice to what the author is trying to say.

What was the most enjoyable?

Spending time with my characters. Also, finding out what happened next. I will always be grateful to the characters of all my novels for allowing me to spend a part of my day with them in their world.

What are your goals for writing fiction?

To write a good story. I believe fiction should entertain and at the very least transport the reader to another world. It should perhaps inspire the reader to make beneficial changes in their own life or even in the world. A teacher of mine in the early grades explained to the class that fiction is a search for the truth. I have always held onto that because I believe in it. But, to echo the words of a writer promoting his book on a TV ad I wouldn't be doing my job if I didn't move you.

Other novels by Jan Surasky

*Rage Against
the
Dying Light*

Back to Jerusalem

*The Lilac Bush
is
Blooming*

www.jansurasky.com

Jan Surasky has worked as a book reviewer, movie reviewer and entertainment writer for a San Francisco daily newspaper. Her many articles and short stories have been published in national and regional magazines and newspapers. She has also taught writing at a literary center and a number of area colleges near her home in upstate New York. Her novel *Rage Against the Dying Light* was an Eric Hoffer Book Award finalist for Fiction. Her novel *Back to Jerusalem* was the Eric Hoffer Book Award winner for Fiction and Grand Prize finalist and the Pacific Book Awards winner for New Fiction. Her novel *The Lilac Bush is Blooming* was the Pacific Book Awards winner for Fiction, a Hollywood Book Festival finalist for Fiction, and a San Francisco Book Festival finalist for Fiction.

www.ingramcontent.com/pod-product-compliance
Lightning Source LLC
Chambersburg PA
CBHW050544260626
47157CB00002B/426